A MURDER OF CROWS

A Saugatuck Murder Mystery

by

G Corwin Stoppel

❖

Lord Hiltensweiller Press

THE SAUGATUCK MURDER MYSTERY SERIES

The Great Saugatuck Murder Mystery

Death by Palette Knife

A Murder of Crows

Copyright ©2018 by G Corwin Stoppel

First Edition

Published by Lord Hiltensweiller Press, Saugatuck, Michigan, 49453
lordhilt@gmail.com

Cover design by S. Winthers

All rights reserved. No part of this book may be reproduced without formal permission.

ISBN-13: 978-1986798372

ISBN-10: 1986798372

*In deepest appreciation to the White and
Phelps families and their employees at
Saugatuck's famous Butler Restaurant*

I am deeply indebted to some wonderful and encouraging friends. Thank you to John Thomas and Professor Peter Schakel for proof-reading and making some truly helpful suggestions; to Maggie Baker Conklin who gave sound advice on the chemical formulas; to Sally Winthers who took the manuscript and converted it into a novel.

Above all, thank you to my wonderful wife Pat Dewey who planted the seeds which led to the mystery.

A MURDER OF CROWS

FORWARD

This is the third book in what has become the Saugatuck Murder Mystery Series. If you have not yet read *The Great Saugatuck Murder Mystery* and *Death by Palette Knife*, you might enjoy them. Many of the major characters were introduced in the first one; others came in the second. Like the first two books, this story is set in Saugatuck, Michigan in the 1920s.

And, like the first two stories, this is a absolute fiction, but don't let that stop you from enjoying it! The characters are also complete works of fiction, and if you think otherwise, you are sadly mistaken. If you even think that there is some resemblance to a real person, living or dead, that is your imagination working over time.

— Spring 2018
  G Corwin Stoppel

A MURDER OF CROWS

CHAPTER ONE

There was a rustling in the crown of an elm tree that shaded the sidewalk off Hoffman Street, just a few steps down the hill from the Congregational Church. It sounded like a squirrel had jumped from one branch to another, missed, and made a valiant effort to catch a lower one, only to miss again. The noise came closer, ending with a heavy thud on the sidewalk. If Phoebe Walters and Jane Bird had taken one more step on their walk home from school it might have landed squarely on their heads.

Both girls let out a long discordant shriek of terror and ran a few yards down the street toward the library before giggling at how frightened they had been, and turned around to look at it. When they came closer they saw it was a crow on the ground.

"It isn't moving," Jane observed in a reverential voice. "Do you think it's dead?"

Phoebe nodded. The eyes were glazed-over, one of them lifelessly staring up at them.

They looked down in pity at the beautiful bird, surprised that its feathers were so black some along the wing seemed almost purple. "It's so sad," Jane whispered. They were interrupted by two more crows tumbling down, both landing just a few feet apart on Mrs. Perkin's lawn.

That was enough for the girls. One crow falling from the sky was frightening; three crows falling in quick succession was terrifying A quick glance at each other, the briefest nod of the head, and they grabbed each other's hand to rush down the street. It was only when they were in the next block that Phoebe panted, "We should tell someone." Jane agreed, adding, "We should. It might be important. Let's go into Koening's Hardware."

The young man behind the counter heard their story and shrugged with disinterest. "Saves shooting them. That's about all any crow is good for. Target practice. They eat a farmer's grain and make a mess, and they're not good for eating. Just target practice." Realizing they were not going to persuade him to take an interest, they went across the street to the Maplewood Hotel.

The two girls waited several long minutes until Bobbie looked up from the telephone switchboard. "Nothing I can do about it right now, girls. I'm on duty, so you best run along," was her only advice.

It was futile. None of the adults in town seemed the least bit interested in three dead crows. Nor, for that matter, later that evening, did Phoebe get much sympathy from her mother. "Everything dies, dear," she sighed. "It's part of life. And before you ask, no, you may not hold a funeral for a dead crow. Not even if there are three of them." She let out a long sigh, "And grading these papers will be the early death of me."

"They might have been a family," Phoebe said quietly. Harriet gave her the mothers' infamous 'That Look' which meant the topic was concluded.

A very sad and frustrated Phoebe went to bed earlier than usual that night, still mourning the crow that nearly hit her, and its two dead companions. Adults didn't seem to care when it was a wild animal. They were different if it was a dog or a cat that was a family pet. Mrs. Colfax had been in mourning for days after her canary died, and asked the minister of her church if he would at least pray for the bird's soul. Adults just weren't interested in a crow.

Sleep did not come easily or quickly to Phoebe as she turned the afternoon's events over in her mind. Maybe her teacher would be interested. Maybe some of her classmates would care. They didn't. By the next morning, even Jane had lost interest in the incident. "Don't be silly," she cautioned.

That afternoon Phoebe walked home alone from school, pausing in front of Mrs. Perkin's house to see if the crows were still on the grass, but they were gone. Someone must have taken them away. She walked on, and an idea came to her. If none of the grown-ups in Saugatuck were interested, perhaps there was one person who was different. When she got home she carefully pulled out a piece of wide-ruled paper from her notebook and began to write. She gave a careful, detailed account of what she had seen, knowing that facts were important, and then asked for advice.

When she finished her letter it occurred to her that if one letter was good, two were even better. She wrote a second message, the thoughts and words coming easier this time. There were envelopes and stamps in her mother's roll top desk, and she had permission to use them whenever she had an important letter to write. And, this was important! Really and truly important! She sealed the envelopes and licked the stamps, pressing them down hard so they wouldn't fall off.

The Regulator wall clock in the dining room assured her that if she hurried she could make it to the Post Office with three minutes to spare. Even though she had joined the Girl Scouts for just a month or so before having enough of it and quitting, she remembered their leader saying that girls should always run ten steps, walk ten steps, and repeat. That way they could get to their destination without getting tired. This was the time to see if it worked!

She made it with time to spare, and the Postmaster told her the letters would go out in the mailbag that night. "Up to Holland, down to Chicago, and all the way to where they belong," he smiled.

"I know." Phoebe repeated their motto about neither snow rain heat, nor rain nor snow, nor gloom of night.

"Okay, well, you best run along. I got to get the mailbag ready if it is going out on the train tonight. Be good," the postmaster told her. Adults were always saying that to children. It was either 'be good' or 'be safe'. This time, she didn't mind. Phoebe walked home, two fingers on each hand crossed, hoping someone would take an interest in her story.

CHAPTER TWO

"Dining car's a bit crowded just now," the steward told him. "And I know how you like to sit alone, Doc, but there's just one table left with a seat a couple of tables back. I think the other couple is finishing up and they'll be gone pretty quick. Looks like you can sit with them and the other passenger or wait. Up to you."

He growled under his breath. He was hungry, and he hated waiting. "Thunderation! No, I'll take the seat," he said.

The steward led him down the aisle to the table, and he sat down. "You got your train-legs, Doc, that's for sure. You ever need a job, you just let me know and I'll put in a good word for you with the higher-ups," the steward teased. "Good to see you again, Sir. Always a pleasure to have a real gentleman of the old school aboard. There aren't many of you left." Horace took the menu, wincing at the accidental mention of his advancing age, holding it up in front of his face to stave off conversation with the others as long as possible. To his relief, the couple were paying their bill and would wait for their change. The other, obviously a woman from the appearance of her hands, held up her menu as she was reading it.

"Well, this is a surprise. I rarely see, much less sit with, someone I know in the dining car," a woman's voice said across the table. She paused, "Hello, Doctor Balfour ... Horace."

He recognized the voice. His eyes widened and his lips tightened as he lowered his menu. Across from him was Beatrix Howell, with a faint smile of triumph on her lips. "I was about to come up to your car after lunch to greet you. I would have invited you to join me for lunch, but we both know how much we value our privacy." She paused to place her order with the steward. "But please do stay."

"And how in thunderation did you know I was on the train?" he asked.

"Because, Horace, you are a man of habit. You get restless just sitting still. What do you call it? I think the phrase is, 'Sitting in the waiting room?' You hate being in the waiting room. When we stopped in Winona to take on water you got off to walk up and down the platform. I assume you wanted some solitude from the other passengers so I did not come out to greet you and I believe you are seated in the car ahead of me."

"Very observant of you," Horace answered, both surprised and irritated at seeing her again, and so soon after their recent adventures in Saugatuck.

"Thank you. A medical conference?" she asked, almost coyly. The steward returned to take his order. "They are not serving whitefish. I suggest the Salisbury steak and baked potato."

Horace followed her advice.

After the steward left he repeated her question about a medical conference. "Something like that," he said.

Beatrix's left eye-brow shot up. "I see," she said with a faint smile again. "And yet your brother is not with you, nor is Fred. That's a bit unusual, is it not?"

"Theo? No. And just how do you know Fred isn't in the parlour car?" Horace asked icily. There was something about the way the woman could be so abrupt, asking such probing questions, that always discomforted him. All the more so when they were personal questions.

She almost laughed. "Because, he would have come with you to the dining car. You might believe yourself to be an aristocrat; well, truth be told, you are one, yet even though Fred is your employee, you treat him as a friend, at times almost an equal. You have a symbiotic relationship. And, since you answered in the singular, you just told me you are travelling alone. That is highly unusual for you. Are you staying long in Chicago?"

Before he could answer her question the other couple excused themselves and left the table. A young steward, still not having 'train legs', swooped in to clean away their dishes, bumped against Horace twice, and apologized profusely. The brief interruption gave him a chance to form his answer.

"For a while, yes. I'm getting off there," he told her.

"Of course you are, but that is not a real answer. The Empire Builder terminates in Chicago. All of us will be getting off there. But after that ... ?" she probed again.

"Well, I have some business to attend to," he said, eager for his meal to arrive so he could stop this conversation.

"Well-said for an oblique answer. I believe, however, your destination is Saugatuck," Beatrix said.

"And what in the world makes you think that?" he asked.

"In fact, I am very certain of it. You see, I received a letter from your granddaughter about the mysterious death of three crows. She wanted my advice as a pathologist. I am very certain it would have been the second letter she wrote. The first, naturally, and rightfully so, would have been to you. The opportunity to see her again would be irresistible for you, and I knew you would go there. When I saw you on the platform in Winona, it confirmed that I was right, although I did not initially expect we would be on the same train. And, since you are right-handed, I believe the letter is still in the left breast pocket of your suit. I cannot imagine how many times you have read and re-read it.

"You received it several days ago, thought it over, and realized it was a perfect justification to make a quick visit to see Phoebe and Harriet before the weather turns cold. You decided to visit her, and yet you have had second thoughts about it. Am I right so far?" Beatrix asked.

"So far," he said with resignation. She was right. He had leapt at the idea of going to see Phoebe again, but moments after the train departed, he was regretting his rashness.

"Good. I like to be right. Since Theo and Clarice were in Saugatuck just a few months ago, they did not want to return so soon. Clarice, I am sure, suggested it would be a wonderful opportunity for you to spend some time with Phoebe on your own. The only challenging question I cannot answer is why Fred is not accompanying you."

It was Horace's turn to smile. "Fred is with some army buddies up near Brainerd at a place called Breezy Point. Bill Fawcett built it a year or so ago, and invited them to come up for a reunion."

"Captain William Fawcett or, Captain Billy, as he prefers to be called. Yes, I know of him, but not personally, of course. I think you told me this summer he wrote for the *Stars and Stripes* newspaper during the war and then began publishing that degenerate magazine which is where he made his money. So yes, little wonder that he would invite his cronies to come up to the resort he built," she said with disdain.

"The *Whiz Bang* is not something I would choose to read, either," Horace said flatly.

"So, to return to my observations. You are travelling alone …"

"Yes, but you're also on a train and not flying," he reminded her, hoping to turn the conversation.

"This time of the year the weather is too problematic. I could always put down on land ahead of a storm and wait it out, but I am not comfortable flying over ninety miles of open water this time of the year."

To his relief, Horace saw the steward coming down the aisle with his meal, and they ate in silence. When she finished first Beatrix unceremoniously announced that she was returning to her seat.

The steward returned, asking if Doctor Horace wanted a cup of tea or coffee, "or something to warm you up, if you get my drift. Chef's got something that might hit the spot." He ran his right index finger over the side of his nose. "It's not my place to be saying it, but …"

"If it is about Doctor Howell, then don't say it. I've known her for years. Yes, please tell the chef I'll take his recommendation. She can be frosty at times."

"Just the ticket to take the chill off," the steward said, rubbing his index finger across his nose, and then winking.

He returned with a cup of amber liquid. "More of that where it came from, if you know what I mean," he said, again rubbing his finger across his nose. "He could refill your hip flask if you're running low. Some fellas like to have a little nip up in the cars."

The Empire Builder pulled slowly into Union Station, a quarter-hour ahead of schedule, giving Beatrix and Horace over three hours to wait in the Great Hall for the Pere Marquette that would take them to Michigan. Despite the vast size of the room, the two spotted each other, and Beatrix beckoned Horace over to join her on one of the benches.

She continued her conversation from an hour earlier in the dining car, right where she had left off. "What I cannot understand is why Phoebe would take such an interest in a murder of three crows."

"She didn't write about them being murdered. At least not to me," Horace answered, quickly.

"That's what a group of crows is called. A flock of lambs, a pack of wolves, a congress of owls, or in England, a parliament of owls, and so on. Interestingly, a worm of robins, no doubt attributable to their favorite meal. For crows, a group is called a murder. Why would she be so concerned about three dead crows that she would write to both of us? That is something I do not understand, yet," Beatrix said quietly, her eyes looking down. Her tone of voice almost seemed as if she considered her lack of knowledge a failure.

"Because she is a young impressionable girl, and she has a heart …"

"Of course she has a heart," Beatrix replied.

"She has, well, then compassion, feelings, sentimental emotions. She saw three crows fall dead out of the sky and felt sorry for them," Horace said with a slight chuckle. "It wouldn't surprise me if she and her friends haven't already held a funeral for them. Girls at that age are sometimes romanticists."

Beatrix thought it over and said softly, "I do not believe I was that way when I was her age."

Horace thought better than to agree with her. "To tell you the truth, I'm not all that interested in her dead crows. It was just a good excuse to see my granddaughter again. What I can't understand is why she dragged you into this as well."

"She did not. She wanted advice, and her letter merely appealed to my sense of adventure and curiosity. I had just finished a project and was at loose ends. A short jaunt seemed like a good idea to clear out the mental fog."

Horace couldn't help but wonder if perhaps she knew, or at least hoped, he would be in Saugatuck, as well. If she did, then the idea flattered him and frightened him at the same time.

They sat in awkward silence until Horace asked, "Where are you staying?"

"I had wanted to stay at the Colonial, but now that the tourist season is over they are working on some of the rooms. The idea of a guesthouse was not appealing, so I will be at the Butler Hotel. And you? I assume it will be with Mrs. Walters and your granddaughter."

"No. I didn't tell them I was coming. So, the Butler. That's where I am staying, too."

Beatrix stared across the room, thinking it over. "We must be certain that our rooms are at opposite ends of the corridor so that people do not have the wrong idea and talk. We will have been travelling together; it could happen."

"No, we certainly wouldn't want that, now would we? Perhaps we should see if we had rooms on separate floors," Horace said, trying not to smile. He turned to reach for his bag to extract a book.

"Sherlock Holmes?" Beatrix asked.

"No, not this time. Some new author. A patient gave it to me. It's by some woman named Christie. Agatha Christie."

"I have not heard of her."

"She's English. So far, it seems quite good. The odd thing is she has a Belgian fellow as the detective. Frankly, I don't think it will ever catch on over here."

"A Belgian detective does not seem as odd as three elderly physicians solving a murder, and I am quite certain they have crime in

Belgium." She dropped the subject to pull out the recent edition of the *New Yorker* magazine and began reading. Both of them read for an hour or so, until Horace announced he would return in a few minutes, and Beatrix agreed to watch over his bag, coat, and walking stick. It was the silver-headed one, with the hidden sword. Perhaps, she thought, he was expecting more excitement than just a few days with his granddaughter.

It was just after he left that a Western Union boy came into the waiting room. "Telegram for Doctor Balfour! Telegram for Doctor Balfour!" he shouted as he strode quickly through the room. Beatrix motioned for him to come over to where she was sitting. "He is travelling with me, and indisposed at the moment," she explained as she signed his ledger for the envelope and tipped him with a fifty-cent piece. The lad's eyes opened wide in appreciation, and he thanked her three times for her generosity, turning around one final time to touch the bill of his cap.

"How did they find you here?" Beatrix asked as Horace opened the envelope.

"I suspect with very little difficulty. It's from Chief Garrison in Saugatuck," he chuckled. "Well, from the looks of it, my guess is he sent it up to me, and young Bill Hornseth at the Western Union must have heard from his father at the hardware that I was going to Saugatuck. He sent it on to Chicago, and here it is. A bit roundabout."

Beatrix screwed up her face as if she had just eaten something very sour. "I am not certain I would like everyone being privy to my affairs. Please tell me that nothing has happened to Harriet or Phoebe," she said in a strained voice.

"No. Not at all. They're both all right. According to Garrison, he wants me to come quickly because there's been a murder." He handed the message to Beatrix so she could read it.

When she returned it to him she said, "Well, she has certainly been thorough to ask the police chief to investigate three dead crows."

"Well, we'll find out when we get there. Maybe, now that the tourist season is over, the chief is short on work to keep himself busy. Maybe the murder of crows was murdered after all." He chuckled at his own joke. Beatrix did not find the pun humorous.

The train stopped in Holland long enough to let Beatrix, Horace, and the other passengers get off and collect their bags. Most of them were greeted by waiting family and friends, and soon left the platform. Horace grimaced, saddened and envious of the others, who had their own welcoming committee. It had been a long time since anyone other than Fred had seen him off or welcomed him home. A taxi took the two doctors to Saugatuck, letting them out in front of the Butler. Horace had just paid the driver and looked at the hotel. "Moments like this I miss the *Aurora*," he said softly, thinking about the familiarity of his own cabin and his own bed. Just then, Chief Garrison pulled up behind them, flashed the car lights to get their attention, and jumped out of the car.

"Say, you got here in record time. Guess you got my telegram all right. But, say, I just sent it around ten this morning. Guess you two flew down or something. Never mind all that. It's good to see you. We got us another murder!" The chief pumped Doctor Horace's hand to greet him, completely ignoring Beatrix. "Good to have you here. But I can't understand how you got here so fast."

"Well, my granddaughter Phoebe sent me a letter a couple of days ago," Horace began. "And, in case you don't realize it, this is Doctor Howell standing in front of you. I'm sure you remember her from this summer."

"I received a letter, as well. She reported a murder of crows was found dead," Beatrix added.

The chief screwed up his face. "Lady, what are you talking about? Nobody murdered any crows, not as far as I know. You're confused, lady. We got an old lady murdered."

"A murder of crows is a proper way of describing a flock of them. Phoebe wrote that three of them had died suddenly and one quite literally fell out of the sky at her feet," Beatrix said.

"I don't care about a bunch of dead crows, murdered or not. We've got…"

Beatrix interrupted him again. "It isn't 'murdered' of crows. Simply, 'murder.'"

Horace reached over to put his hands on Beatrix' arm, startling her and she pulled back. "Another time. He's falling behind and I think you are confusing him. Let's hear out the chief. Start again, would you?"

"Like I've been saying, we got us a murder. Now, I didn't send for you, Doctor Howell, but I'm glad you came here anyways in case Doc Balfour needs your help. Say, this is right up your alley. The victim is an older lady who pretty much kept to herself, if you know the type. She's got three knives sticking out of her back. I could use some help figuring out who did it and why. No family, no money, and no suspects. And, you got your work cut out for you because from the looks of it, she's been dead a couple of days. We got her on ice over to a fish house, but she isn't going to keep much longer, if you get my drift. You two did alright this summer, so it seems natural to call you in now seeing as how you're already here."

"Now, just to be clear, you have a human body with three knife wounds, and this has nothing to do with dead crows. Am I right?" Doctor Horace asked.

"Now you're talking, Doc. Dead lady with three knives in her back. Far as I'm concerned a dead crow is the only good type of crow there is, and I'm not interested in them. Noisy, filthy things. It's the old lady I'm interested in. Now, I'll bet you want to come along and take a look at the body, and get started right away. Won't take but a couple of minutes to drive over for a look-see. Like I said, we got her in the cold room over to one of the fish shacks along the river."

"Not tonight," Horace yawned. "Doctor Howell and I've had a very long day riding on two trains. I won't speak for her, but I'm tired. So, I'm going to register, get my key, and turn in. If she has been dead this long, then we can make a fresh start of it in the morning. That's when we'll decided whether we're getting involved. Maybe those dead crows aren't of interest to you, but they are to my granddaughter Phoebe, and that's good enough for me, and so far, that's the only reason I'm here. We'll see what tomorrow brings."

"You want to have a look-see before you turn in, Doctor Howell?" the chief offered.

"No thank you. I do not think examining a murder victim this late in the evening would be conducive to my sleep. Tomorrow will be better," she also yawned.

"You sure? I figured you'd be curious, you being a woman who's a doctor and all," the chief offered. Beatrix glared at him in disgust. "Just thought you might be curious, that's all," he answered.

"Tomorrow will be better, say around nine?" Horace insisted.

The chief nodded, disappointed that they were uninterested in seeing the body. "Thought you might be interested, that's all," he whined.

"We are. But it will wait until tomorrow when we're rested and there is better light," Horace said firmly.

"You want two rooms?" the night clerk asked from behind the counter.

"Yes, two rooms. Doctor Howell and I are medical colleagues — only," Horace told the young man. "Two rooms, preferably at opposite ends of the hallway, if you have them."

"Guess one of you must snore pretty loud," he chuckled. "Well, it's up to you. Two rooms it is, then. You decide who wants the front of the house. It doesn't matter much to me."

"I would prefer the back, off the street, where it is quieter, if that is all right with you, Doctor," Beatrix said firmly.

"This time of year it's quiet everywhere. I'll call the bellboy to carry up your bags."

Beatrix held out her hand for the key. "I am perfectly capable on my own. Thank you, just the same." Her feathers were still ruffled from the chief's rude comments; the deskman had only made her more irritable. She was already walking toward the stairs before Horace finished signing the registration book. She waited for him on the landing.

"I saw you out front talking with the police. You two aren't wanted or something, are you?" the clerk asked. "We don't want no funny stuff going on here."

Horace chuckled. "No, not at all. We're here about a murder of crows." He enjoyed the puzzled look on the young man's face.

The two of them walked up the stairs. "Horace," Beatrix said, "thank you."

"For what?" he asked, puzzled at what she meant.

"For your respect."

He was still puzzled, but thanked her.

CHAPTER THREE

Phoebe and her mother were ready to sit down at the breakfast table when Horace knocked on the front door. "It's probably Jane or one of your friends wanting to walk to school. Go and answer it, please. Or, maaaaaaybeeee it's that nice young man, Henry who is so sweet on you," Harriet teased.

"Mother!" Phoebe said with disgust, rolling her eyes for emphasis. She turned quickly before she began to blush.

She opened the door and for a moment stared up in stunned silence at her grandfather. "I believe this is where a hug is in order," he teased, bending down to pick her up as she wrapped her arms around his neck and gave him a kiss on his left cheek. He set her down again and they walked hand in hand back to the kitchen. "Don't tell Mother about the letter. Not just yet, jake?" she whispered. He looked surprised, quite certain the girl would have told her mother about it, but whispered back, "Jake with me." It was an unsettling beginning.

Harriet was at the sink, allowing Horace a moment of fun while her back was turned. "Excuse me, ma'am, I just got into town late last night and was wondering if you could use a handyman in return for a decent meal" She wheeled around, staring at him.

"Horace! What are you doing here?"

"Oh, I thought I might come by to see if my best girl is keeping up with her piano lessons. You know, check up on my investment in her music career, and see if it is paying dividends yet. The other day I was thinking we ought to book Carnegie Hall next year if she's up to snuff, so I thought I ought to find out for myself. Besides, I've never seen Saugatuck when it wasn't full of tourists. Now seemed like a good time to do it."

Harriet dried her hands on her apron and untied it, tossing it over the back of a chair. Her eyebrows knitted in worry. "Horace, is there something you're not tell me? Are you alright? What's wrong?" Her voice was strained and anxious.

"Trust me on this, but there is nothing wrong. Absolutely nothing. I promise you. I was getting a bit restless rattling around in that big house after our adventures here, and decided to do something on the spur of the moment. That's all. I thought it might be a surprise. I hope it's a good one."

"The only surprise is you doing something spontaneously. Spur of the moment, my eye! Did Theo and Clarice come with you?" she asked eagerly.

"No, I decided to come on my own. They're still back home. And before you ask, Fred went to a Doughboy reunion, so like I said, I was rattling around a big empty house on my own for long enough. I thought I'd drop in to see you two, maybe have some whitefish and go back in a day or so," he said. "Any chance for coffee here?"

"Horace, you are holding something back, and I know it. If you were younger, I'd say you ran away from home. And your timing right now is horrible. Phoebe and I have to get to school, so whatever it is, it's going to have to wait. I'm sorry, but that's the way it is. Now, you will be having dinner here this evening, won't you? 'No' is not an acceptable answer. Tell me you will come, and then you will tell me everything."

"Of course," he smiled.

"And you are staying here, aren't you? We want you to. Phoebe can move into my room with me and you can have her bedroom," Harriet said.

"Well, I've already checked in at the Butler and paid for a couple of nights."

"But can't you check out and then move here, Grandfather?"

"We'll see. I'll go all the way to 'maybe' on that idea. No promises. Let's just wait, shall we?"

Harriet glanced at the clock. "Phoebe, now get your things and take a sweater with you in case it gets cold by the time school is out. I have a meeting, so you'll be walking home. Remember to bring your books and homework! And, remember your lunch. And you, Horace, back here at five o'clock for dinner, right?"

"Yes, Ma'am," he said with a deep bow.

"You could invite someone to join us for dinner," Phoebe suggested, very obviously fishing for more information.

"We'll see. That is, if it is alright with your mother. I might be able to scrounge up someone who could do with a good meal. Let's see, you've already met a few bootleggers and forgers, so that's no fun. Maybe a highwayman, safe-cracker, bank robber. You know, someone interesting. Say, how about a retired stage coach bandit? I wonder if there are any of them in town this time of the year?"

Both women stared at him, their mouths open. Phoebe was delighted at the prospect of having a gangster over for dinner; Harriet was not. She tightened her lips and gave him a glare over the top of her glasses.

"Oh, Mother! Grandfather was only teasing," Phoebe sighed.

It was only when they were in Harriet's Ford driving toward the school that she told her daughter, "Now, if you know what's going on, you'd better tell me right this very minute. Is that clear, young lady? Your grandfather didn't just turn up here on a whim. I doubt he has ever done anything on a whim. Something is going on, and I think you either know about it or have a hand in it."

"I'm just as surprised as you are, Mother."

"Phoebe Walters, I'm serious. So help me, you'll be grounded for a week if you are holding out!"

"Mother, everything is alright. Grandfather just said he decided to come for a visit, that's all. You heard him, same as me."

"And did he have a bit of encouragement? From you?" she asked.

"Well, maybe. Just a little. I wrote to him about the dead crows, but that's it. I didn't *really* ask him to come," she answered slowly, carefully choosing her words.

"You wrote to him about those dead crows, and he just turned up all of a sudden? Phoebe, you'll be grounded for a month if I find out you made him come down here just for some dead birds. Your grandfather may be retired, but he's still taking care of people. He's your grandfather, but he is a very important man. Really! The idea!"

Harriet waited for some children crossing Butler Street on their way to school, and happened to glance over at the sidewalk in front of Whipple's Grocery Store. She stared at a woman who was walking down the street, her arms straight down at her sides, looking straight ahead. "Did you happen to hear an aeroplane yesterday or early this morning?"

Phoebe froze in fear. "No," she said softly. "Why do you ask? Did you?" Her mother knew something and wasn't telling her.

"No. No, neither did I. But doesn't that woman over there look remarkably like Doctor Howell? How unusual. Do you think it's a coincidence that your grandfather *and* Doctor Howell arrived here at the same time? I wonder if they know the other is here, or maybe that's another coincidence."

"I wouldn't know. We really haven't studied coincidences in school yet," Phoebe fibbed.

"I see. Well, this is going to be a very interesting dinner tonight. I have lots of questions, and I'm sure I'll think of a few more during the day. I'm looking forward to it, aren't you?"

Phoebe felt queasy, knowing that her mother was onto her. She blurted out the first thing that came to mind, "Maybe they have something important to tell us," and instantly regretted it.

"No. The two of them together? No. That's utterly impossible. It would never happen," she said, almost desperately hoping she was right. Harriet's throat felt tight, her stomach doing a summersault. What if Phoebe was right?

The girl's reprieve came unexpectedly, and she was grateful for it even though she didn't like the reason nor how it happened. Phoebe and her mother were probably the only two people in Saugatuck and Douglas who hadn't already heard about the murder of Caroline LeBeau. The whole town was talking about it, including all of Phoebe's school mates as they lined up and waited for the morning bell before marching two by two into the building. Phoebe knew she should feel sad for the poor woman, even if she didn't know her, but for the moment she was relieved. If there had to be bad news, at least the timing could not have been better.

"That was close," she whispered to herself, wiping the back of her right hand over her forehead.

Beatrix was waiting in the hotel dining room, a cup of coffee in front of her. "What have you decided?" she asked when Horace joined her. "You must have awakened early and gone for a walk to think it over. Are you going to pursue this murder case or your granddaughter's crows?" she asked. "Or both?"

"I'm of half a mind to stay out of it. The murder, that is. You heard the chief last night saying how we helped him arrest John Reynolds, or Giovanni Renaldi, as it turned out, last summer. Helped! Thunderation! We caught him fair and square, risked our lives, and now he's taking all the credit. Why should I get involved? We, that is. Why should we do all the legwork? Besides, he was rude to you last night."

"First, to be completely accurate, he did make the arrest, so he was right on that count. All we did was hold him until the chief arrived. And second," Beatrix leaned closer to him, "the truth is that Reynolds caught us, remember? We walked into an ambush and could have been killed. But, yes, I was also offended by his comment, even if he was technically correct."

"So we agree. We're not getting involved, right?" Horace asked.

Beatrix flashed a rare smile. "You know very well that you cannot resist a mystery. And, to be truthful, neither can I." She paused to look away. "Horace, you and I are both retired, put out to pasture like a couple of old work horses when we know we've got plenty of life left in us. We can still pull our weight; Theo, too, for that matter. These youngsters keep us around just because they feel sorry for the 'poor old dears,' but they cannot wait for us to fall off our perches and get out of their way. So, no, I do not think we are just going to walk off into the sunset. At least not yet. Let us put our egos back in our pockets and think of it as a way of keeping our minds working. Besides, since you are still taking Royal Jelly, it should be an easy case to solve. I believe some of your less savory friends would say, 'easy to crack.'"

"I prefer Emile Coue's motto: 'In each and every way, I'm getting better and better each and every day.' Or something like that, anyway. And yes, I am still taking that nostrum you gave me."

"So, we are in," she said firmly. "That is settled." She flashed a wintery smile at him and took a sip of coffee.

"Thunderation! You're right. We're in!"

"On one condition. Horace, I insist you promise that we are not going to get ambushed. Looking down the business end of a gun is a highly over-rated experience. Once was enough. It is a very disquieting experience. Will you promise?"

"I promise to do my best not to get surprised by a fiend with a gun."

"That is all you are promising?" she demanded.

"As good as it gets," he told her.

"Fine! That is acceptable to me. We are in. I am sure that will be of great comfort to Chief Garrison." Beatrix almost giggled.

"So, that's the way we found her out to her place. Face down, just like this, probably dead for at least a day, maybe a day and a half," Chief Garrison said as Doctor Landis pulled down the sheet that draped the body. "When I sent for you, I remembered how you figured out the knife wound in that fellow out at Ox-Bow, and thought you might help me out again."

Horace's lips tightened and it was all he could do to stop from asking, "Help you out again?" And, just what had Garrison done solving the murder of a man with a pallet knife sticking out of his heart? Nothing! The chief was on the wrong track from the beginning, thinking it was a robbery gone wrong. All he wanted to do was keep it quiet so it wouldn't hurt the tourist business. They did all the work and he took all the credit.

Horace kept his tongue.

The three men watched as Beatrix bent over the body for a closer examination. Garrison continued, "From the handles, they appear to be fish knives that most of the fellows along the river carry. Filet knives. They keep them sharp as anything, so it wouldn't take much effort to do her in. Three different handles, but all the same type of knife. Commercially made, not some shank made by a cabin boy. Looks to me like three people killed her. I wouldn't be surprised if they were stolen from a fishing shack. Some of those fellows can be pretty rough characters, but none of them seem the type to kill someone, unless they get liquored up and start fighting. Anyway, I've got one of my fellows looking into it."

Beatrix ignored the conversation, focusing on the body, slowly walking around the stretcher to see it from all angles. She continued staring at the body, saying nothing, as she leaned closer to study it for a few moments, then stepped back again and moved to a different angle.

She stood up, putting her hands on her lower back to stretch for a moment or two. "I trust you have taken photographs and blood samples?" she asked.

"Done on both counts," Garrison told her. "I took the film myself over to the pharmacy and we should have it back later today. Newspaper could have done it quicker, but I wanted to keep this on the QT until we know what's what."

"And I had the blood samples sent to the university hospital over to Ann Arbor with orders for a thorough analysis. Good thing I did, seeing as how you're here, Doctor Howell," Doctor Landis nervously chuckled.

She ignored what was intended to be a compliment to her expertise as a pathologist. "Then perhaps we can remove the knives and turn the body over on her back. I would encourage you to be careful not to smear any fingerprints when you remove them."

Garrison and Horace removed the knives, the chief telling her that they'd already looked for prints, setting them aside, and the three men rolled the body over. Beatrix began examining her face for several minutes, wincing in pain as she stood up again.

"Well?" Garrison asked.

"I believe she was already face down on the ground when she was stabbed." She pointed to the woman's chin and forehead.

"That bruising might be the result of the blood pooling from the way she was left on the floor, on this stretcher or from a blow itself," Doctor Landis said.

"I agree. But right now I am not interested in the bruising. Notice the slight abrasions on her forehead, chin, and nose. Observe also the abrasions on her right cheekbone. The victim was either pushed or fell down, maybe collapsed, but I doubt she was held down, and then stabbed. Or, she may have tripped over something and fell down on her own. There is no real way of telling until we get a report on her blood. That may tell us something useful. I assume you took samples from under her fingernails?"

"Just some dirt, and that was about it," Landis said. "And before you ask, nothing foreign in her mouth or throat, either."

"And you examined her for, for, any sort of intimate violation?"

"If you're asking if we examined, the answer is no. Nothing we could do with the knives in her back. When we get the body back to the hospital, then we can do it," Doctor Landis said.

Once again, Beatrix ignored the conversation, following her own line of thought. "Until we get a blood work up we will not know much more. I believe Doctor Balfour and I should see the scene of the crime." She turned to Horace and asked, "Agreed?"

"That should be our next stop," he said. "That, and looking at the Certificate of Death."

"Well, I don't think you're going to like it very much," Dr. Landis said, looking down at his feet, embarrassed.

"Why is that?" Horace asked.

"Outside of her name and address and the still very preliminary probable cause and date of death, there isn't much I could fill in. We have no idea when or where she was born, next of kin, or much of anything else. Right now, even the exact cause of death is unknown, but you already know that. Most of the certificate is still blank. Doctor, we're in a small town; it's different than if we had your resources."

"Education? Occupation?" Horace asked. He paused and looked at Landis, "You don't even know when she was born, you said? Was she your patient? You must have some records."

"I never saw her professionally. It's a small town, so yeah, I saw her around. I heard she worked at some of the guesthouses as a cleaner, and at a couple of stores years back, but that's about it. I know she stocked shelves and cleaned at the drug store for a while, and then the grocery, but I'm pretty sure it was well before my time. But, beyond that, well, I couldn't be sure. She never came into my office, so no, I wouldn't have any medical records."

"Thunderation!" Horace exploded.

"And, you might as well know, no one has come forward to claim the body. I'd heard she was a Frenchie so I figured she must have been a Catholic, but the priest at St. Pete's over to Douglas never knew of her. None of the other preachers know about her, either, for that matter," Chief Garrison said, bracing himself for the inevitable blast from Horace.

"Thunderation! No one knows anything."

Beatrix was calmer and stayed focused. "I assume you bought the practice from your predecessor, and would have retained his or her records…"

"His," he answered.

"So, the question becomes, did you retain his records, and perhaps those of his predecessor?"

"Probably. All the old ledgers would be down in the basement of the hospital if they still exist. And I have no idea what shape they're in. The mice might have gotten into them," he told her. "Nor if they're complete, much less accurate."

"I see. Then that is where you might want to start, Chief Garrison," she said quietly. To everyone's surprise, she was no longer interested in their conversation. She turned on her heals and returned to examining the body, bending over it to carefully and methodically inspecting the woman's hands. When she stood up there was the mere hint of a smile on her lips. Horace understood she had found something. She resumed her examination.

Chief Landis broke the silence. "So, we're supposed to look at a lot of medical files on the off-chance that maybe, just maybe, the deceased was once a patient of some doctor in the past? Well, how much time is that going to take? Any idea? It's a pretty tall order, if you ask me. Besides, you doctors make chicken scratchings look legible. And then, after all that, you want to go look at her house. Well, I'll tell you, my boys and I were out there, and the only thing worth seeing are the chalk marks we put around the body before we took her out of there. Well, you don't even have to go out there to do that. Soon as I have the photographs developed you can see it in black and white," the chief snarled.

Beatrix finished examining Miss or Mrs. LeBeau's hands, and answered. "Yes, Chief Garrison, you have said it all quite succinctly. Since you express such disinterest, we *are* going through all of the medical files in case she was a patient. And, yes, as Doctor Balfour said, we *are* going to look at the scene of the crime. If you are not capable of doing a thorough investigation, then please stay out of our way and leave it to the two of us." She stood up, her hands on her hips, staring at the chief, rephrasing and repeating herself for emphasis. "I know you are undoubtedly a very busy man, and not an expert in medical records, therefore we will do that ourselves, thank you very much. And, without interference or being rushed, as I am sure you will understand.

"And, we will want to look at her house," Doctor Horace added to emphasize Beatrix's point. He stared down the chief until he finally wilted and agreed.

The four of them left the frigid fish locker, eager to get back outside in the warm sun and much less aromatic air. "Where do you want to start, Horace?" Beatrix asked, still breathing deeply in the fresh air.

"As my daughter-law would say about sorting through papers, 'I hate inventory,' so let's get that done first. Maybe it'll get us somewhere when we see the house," Horace told her.

"My thought, as well. Doctor Landis, if it is convenient, we will start with the files in your basement. By any chance, do you have even an approximate idea when the deceased first came here?" Beatrix asked. "Oh, and first, I believe some antiseptic soap and water is in order when we get there."

He scratched at his right ear, thinking. "For some reason, I don't think it was much before the turn of the century. More likely it was a year or so after that, as I recall. Leastwise, I remember hearing that somewhere. I think I heard that from Mrs. Mae Heath."

"Good, at least that is a start. I know you are about to offer us a ride, but if you do not object, I believe Doctor Balfour and I will walk back to your office. Socrates always proclaimed one does one's best thinking while walking. We have much to consider," she told him. "Or, was it Aristotle? I cannot remember. Philosophy is of little interest to me."

As soon as they were alone, Horace said, "I saw you wince when you stood up."

"It is one of the displeasures of growing old, and Horace, we *are* old. Well, at least getting older. Walking will do me some good," she told him firmly.

"You were examining her hands. Did you find anything?"

"Perhaps. I will not be certain until we see the lab results on blood. If I am right, there is every reason to believe that whoever killed her may have been doing her a favor."

"Poison?" Horace asked.

"I refuse to speculate until I see the report."

"Poison. Well, that would also explain the murder of crows," Horace smiled.

"Please, do not start on that subject again. Not everyone appreciates your sense of humor."

They walked in silence, both thinking, until Horace stated the obvious, "I don't think we're going to get much help out of the chief."

"That is an obvious statement, and I agree. The man is impatient and out of his depth, which explains his contempt for others and his belligerence," Beatrix said as she walked. "I doubt he is a well educated man. And I have some serious doubts about his qualifications as an investigator. Neither he nor Doctor Landis observed the very small amount of blood from the knife wounds, and that is unique." She suddenly stopped and turned toward Horace with a smile. "But it is a delicious mystery, is it not? A woman whose name we may or may not know, no connections with the community in which she has lived for thirty plus years, and no motive. This will be a challenge! Fascinating!" She clapped her hands together several times.

Horace was surprised at her glee.

CHAPTER FOUR

A solitary light bulb, festooned with dangling cobwebs and patina of dust, hung from the basement ceiling beneath Doctor Landis' office. Somehow in the gloom, Horace and Beatrix found the old ledgers, hidden by more cobwebs and more dust. "I imagine this is a bit like opening up King Tut's Tomb," Horace said. A moment later he groaned, leading Beatrix to ask, "What is it?"

"It's an old-fashioned chronological ledger, and I am sure no one ever bothered to cross-reference it. Here, take a look," he told her, holding up the book. "Date, patient's name, and a few brief notes. Next line, next patient and the same thing, and so on. Sometimes it's just an initial. We'll have to go through it line by line."

Beatrix looked at the old book and chuckled, "That takes us back, does it not?"

"It's before my time," Horace told her.

"Horace Balfour, you know better than that. We did the same thing when we were starting out as interns. So, pay for your sins of omission and let us get to work. I am going upstairs to find lab coats to keep the dust off our clothes." When she returned, she handed one to him, "The latest fashion. Now, to work." The only sound was the slow turning of pages.

"Four hours of work, and we don't have much to show for it, do we? One brief memo that a Caroline LeBeau was treated for a broken big toe on her right foot. It doesn't say whether she stubbed it or dropped something on it. Nothing!" Horace yawned in exasperation, ending with muffled "Thunderation!"

"When was it?" Beatrix asked, still looking through old ledgers.

"June 22nd, 1906. Nothing before or since then. I started in 1885, just to be on the safe side. That didn't accomplish anything, did it? Much as I hate to admit it, Garrison might be right about a waste of time. Births, a few stillborns, and a lot of death by drowning, consumption, and old war wounds. Oh, and childbirths. All pretty routine stuff for a small town practice. And, before you ask, I checked by both names and her initials forward and backward."

Beatrix closed the last of the financial ledgers she had examined and returned it to the shelf. "Welcome to my world of forensics. I spend as much time looking at books as through a microscope," she said flatly, not acknowledging his thoroughness. "What we do know is that she had an iron constitution. Either that, or she was like a lot of folks from the old country who just suffered in silence and never saw a doctor until they could not take the pain anymore. On to look at her house?" Beatrix asked as they left Doctor Landis' office, their now gray lab coats unceremoniously tossed into a hamper.

"Nope. Enough is enough for one day. I could use some fresh air or a nap, or both. Besides, Harriet and Phoebe are planning on us joining them for dinner. Say, that reminds me, you're invited, too."

"You just remembered to tell me now? Are you quite sure I am even wanted? I trust you did not tell Harriet that I came in on the train with you. She might get the wrong idea!"

"No, I didn't say a thing about you being here. She said I was to be there at five, and I was welcome to bring a guest. I think Phoebe is hoping I'll bring at least one arch villain, but she'll be much happier to see you again. So will Harriet." he chuckled.

"I hope you are not suggesting I would qualify as a villain," Beatrix said flatly.

"No. No, of course not. But you're a long time friend, and that always makes it even better. As I said, I know Harriet will be happy to see you again. So will Phoebe. Say yes, perhaps we have something light to eat now and get some rest before we go."

"I would think you would rather spend time alone with your family. I will have dinner brought up to my room at the hotel."

"I can appreciate that. But sooner or later they will know you are here, and well, they might feel snubbed if you don't have dinner with them," he explained quietly, giving her time to think about it. Beatrix swallowed hard, and nodded her head. She would go with him.

Despite her discomfort of what seemed like an intrusion, she knew that he was right. To avoid his family would be unacceptable. She nodded silently in agreement a second, then walked as far away as possible from him on the sidewalk, her arms folded over her chest. Horace didn't know if she was focused on their mystery or anxious about dinner. "Can't figure that woman out," he thought to himself.

"I must get a gift for Harriet. Perhaps flowers," she said.

"I'll bet Phoebe would love a set of brass knuckles," he teased.

"Horace," Beatrix said in disgust. "That is inappropriate for a young girl. I will buy flowers to take. Do you know what they will be wearing? I do not want to over or under dress." She shuddered anxiously.

"Oh, something blue," he said.

She stopped abruptly and turned to face him. "I always wear blue."

"Then you're fixed for the evening."

Dinner began with unbridled anxiety and an abundance of caution all around. Beatrix was anxious about dinner with people she felt she barely knew. Even if she had been to Saugatuck several times and studied with Harriet at Ox-Bow, she was uncomfortable and still not certain she was truly welcome or if she had been extended a "pity invitation." Phoebe was worried that her grandfather would bring up the trio of crows and the letter she had sent him. She was even more worried that Beatrix would say something. Harriet was still worried that there was something wrong with Horace's health. Or his finances. Or perhaps something else. Ever since she had seen Beatrix on the street earlier that morning, an even more frightening thought kept running through her mind: What if Horace and Beatrix … ?

It was not until they began eating that Horace was able to relax everyone. "It's a treat having a home cooked meal in a dining room that isn't rocking," he smiled. "Thank you for inviting me, both of us, that is. I suppose you've heard about the murder, which is why Chief Garrison sent for us."

"We did this morning," Harriet said. "I didn't think you came all this way to check up on Phoebe's piano lessons."

"Well, to tell you the truth, not at first. But now that I am here, I'd like to hear all about it. How are you getting along with Miss Hansen, or do I still call her Madame Chopin?" he asked Phoebe.

Both Beatrix and Harriet breathed a sigh of temporary relief, grateful that Horace had changed the subject. "Now, that's an interesting story," Harriet interrupted before her daughter could speak. "As your gangster buddies would say, 'she dropped the dime on teaching piano lessons.'"

"I think the phrase is 'took a powder,' but never mind that. What? When did that happen?" Horace asked.

"I do not understand the meaning of the phrase," Beatrix interrupted.

"It means she quit," he told her quietly. "I'll explain later."

"That, Horace, is all your fault — for which I am surprisingly more than a little grateful. It seems that you and your jazz friends introduced her to performing on stage, and playing ragtime. The first of September, she told all her students that she was quitting, unless they wanted to learn jazz piano. No more classical music; she was done with it. Too old-fashioned. She said it was stodgy and dull. And that's not all. She bought a camera and is taking pictures of all the bands that play in town, hoping to become their piano player and photographer! And if she does leave, we won't have the town poisoner slinging hash next summer at Ox-Bow! Thank goodness for that!"

"Permanently?" Horace asked.

"I believe so. She auditions with every group or singer that comes to town. I think a photographer for one of the Chicago papers who was up here had a lot to do with it. He's gotten a few of them into the city papers. Now, she wants to travel the country as a pianist and photographer."

"So, who is your teacher, Phoebe?" her grandfather asked.

"I have a new teacher, Miss Lila Harrington. She's not as mean as Miss Hansen, but she's just as strict. I still have to practice half an hour every day," the girl pouted.

"She's putting together a glee club, too, but Phoebe doesn't want to join," Harriet added.

"I see," Horace said, giving Phoebe a knowing wink. "You're not taking a vacation from your short wave radio, are you?" Horace asked her.

Her face lit up and she carefully said, "No," trying not to sound too cheerful.

"Good girl! And it's much quieter, too," Horace smiled, giving her a wink. "Meanwhile, what have you two heard about unfortunate Miss LeBeau?"

"Just that she was found dead looking like a porcupine with three knives in her back," Phoebe said, obviously repeating something she had heard at school.

"I'm not certain that dinner is the time to discuss, well, her sudden demise. And Phoebe, it is not respectful to speak of the dead that way. I don't want to hear that sort of talk from you ever again," her mother said firmly.

"I really do not see what is discomforting about it. When I came home on term holidays in medical school, my mother always encouraged me to tell her all I was learning, including autopsies," Beatrix said. "Some of the work was very interesting to her."

Horace ignored her comment and continued, "That seems to be all anyone knows; so far, at least. But what can you tell me about her? Doctor Landis and the police chief didn't know much, but perhaps you knew her or something about her."

"Right now, anything would be helpful," Beatrix told the two women.

"I'm afraid I can't be much help. I mean, I would see her in town once in a while. We all probably did at one time or another. But really, she kept to herself. She was polite and friendly if someone spoke to her, but she wasn't one to start a conversation. Never, at least not as far as I know. I don't think she ever joined any clubs or anything like that. At least, nothing to do with art, or I would have known it. And, she wasn't an Episcopalian, that much I am sure, or I would have seen her at church," Harriet said apologetically.

"The chief said she worked as a cleaner at some of the guest houses. Do you know which ones? Beatrix asked.

"Sorry, no. I heard that too, and that she cleaned and stocked shelves at Whipple's grocery store and at the pharmacy, but I don't recall seeing her there. Look, I am ashamed to be saying this, but she was the sort of mousy little woman who would have blended into the wallpaper. I wish I could be more help. Oh, there are a couple of places you could check for information. Try Bobbie at the switchboard, and then go across the street over to Koening's Hardware. Bobbie would know everything that goes on around here, if anyone does. And, the men who sit around the stove there know more about what's going on than anyone else, even her. And what they don't know, they can make up."

"You have been more helpful than you realize. At least we can start with those two places," Beatrix told them.

"I heard she was a witch!" Phoebe chimed in, her eyes widening. "That's what some of the girls in my class said. She lived all by herself in a little house along the river, and she did black magic. Maybe she flew around town on a broomstick. Does that help?"

Beatrix paused and said, "Perhaps. It is something to keep in mind. The other interesting thing about all of this is that the chief mentioned something about dead crows. There might be a connection to the crows if she was a witch. Thank you for your contribution, Phoebe, it might be vital information," Beatrix told her. "Doctor Balfour, we must take that into consideration."

"Interesting," Horace said quietly. "The chief didn't seem at all interested in talking about the crows. Perhaps there was a reason for that. I wonder if there is a connection. Interesting. Yes, thank you, Phoebe. I think that is something Doctor Howell and I will have to explore a bit further. Right now, anything is helpful."

Harriet coughed, not so much to clear her throat, as to send a clear message that there would be no further talk about murder, dead crows, and witches.

The old physician gave his granddaughter a wink and ran his right finger on the side of his nose. Phoebe's secret was out, and now she didn't have to worry about it anymore because she was helping to solve a crime. "You know, if you decide not to become a Western Union telegraph operator, you might want to become a detective," he told her.

"You would better employ your mind if you became a physician like your grandfather," Beatrix said firmly.

Harriet tried to lighten the mood. "Or, perhaps a mystery writer. With her imagination she might have a successful career."

The dinner which had started out uncomfortably ended in the same fashion. Horace and Beatrix offered to help with the clean up, but Harriet was adamant that she didn't have room for both of them in her kitchen. When he offered a second time she raised her voice to say she would do it herself. "And Phoebe has her homework to do," she reminded them. "You're finally being challenged, aren't you, dear?" she asked her daughter. Twice within the minute Harriet looked at the clock on the wall.

Horace took that as his cue for them to say goodnight. Beatrix was far more relaxed on the walk back to the Butler Hotel, relieved that the evening was over.

"Well, that was ragged, wasn't it?" Horace asked her. Uncertain how to answer, Beatrix said nothing.

"Right now, I wish Fred was here. He's good at talking with people, ferreting and teasing out information, and that sort of thing. Looks to me like we got a lot of that to do," Horace lamented. He didn't need to add that he and Beatrix were the two worst candidates for the task of getting people to warm up to them to reveal secrets.

"You know where he is. I know if you sent him a telegram message he would drop everything to come here," Beatrix suggested.

"I know. I know he would. But, he's having a vacation. It wouldn't be fair to him to call him away like that. I'll send a message to Theo in the morning, asking him to see if Fred can come down here once he gets back home," Horace said. "Well, if he isn't too tired, that is."

"Meanwhile, we have plenty to do," Beatrix said, almost cheerfully. "First thing tomorrow we still need to look at her house, and perhaps poke around town and see if anyone knows anything that would be helpful."

"More helpful than Phoebe telling us her friends think she is a witch?" Horace laughed. "Especially a witch flying around on a broom?"

"I am not so certain. There may be some truth to it," Beatrix said quietly.

Horace stopped and turned toward her. "Are you serious about that?"

"At the moment, it cannot be discounted. Elderly women, living alone on the edge of a village or out in the woods, have always been suspected of practicing witchcraft. I can just imagine the danger I would be in if I lived three hundred years ago. Sometimes the idea of witches is a complete paranoid fantasy; sometimes there may be more truth to it. You will remember the old adage of smoke and fire. Right now, we must keep an open mind. For all we know, that is why she was murdered. It might even explain the dead crows. An open mind to that and anything else! If people did think she really was a witch, perhaps that is why she was murdered." Beatrix resumed walking, and Horace joined her. He was surprised that she had such an open mind to witchcraft.

At the doorway of the hotel he asked, "Coffee at eight in the dining room?"

"Yes. Very good." She paused, then nodded toward a group of leather-covered chairs in the lobby. "Horace I think your wish came true. I believe there is someone here to see you." She pointed to a large chair opposite them.

"Good evening, Boss!" Fred said as he came across the room.

"What in thunderation … ?"

The two men shook hands and Fred began explaining. "Well, it's like this. A day or so ago Doctor Theo sent a telegram up to Captain Billy's place to let me know you'd come down here to Saugatuck, and not to worry about it. I guess he figured I'd want to know, which I did. Well, by then I'd had about enough time up there and was ready to get back to home. Too much drinking and cussing, things like that, for my taste. Some of those boys let themselves go like they were on liberty, if you get my meaning. And a couple of them brought along their daughters. Leastwise, they looked young enough to be their daughters, which I don't think they were, if you get my drift. I figured it was time for what our lieutenant called a 'strategic withdrawal' when the Huns were making things too hot for comfort. Same thing with those boys up to Breezy Point. So, I was real pleased to get his telegram. I got back home that night, and Doc filled me in on the particulars, and here we are. "

"We?" Horace asked. "Who else is here?"

"Hold your horses. I'm getting to that part. You see, it's like this. Just about the last minute when I was getting ready to come down here, Doctor Theo and his missus decided to tag along. Oh, and I brought this along. I figured you must have left your walking stick to home on accident. It's not your special silver headed one, on account of the fact that I couldn't find it, but I brought this one along just in case it might come in handy like it did earlier on." Fred looked down to Horace's right hand. "See you already got it with you." He paused for a moment and said, "Now, you got yourself a back up."

"You mean, Theo and Clarice are here, too?"

"That they are. Doctor Theo just went down the hallway, pardon me for saying so, Doctor Howell, and Mrs. Balfour is already up in their room. He'll be along directly."

"I am truly glad to see you. You remember Doctor Beatrix Howell, of course."

Fred pulled off his hat to greet her.

"Do you have a room yet?"

"Yup, sure do. We got two rooms. One for Doc Theo and Mrs. Theo, and one for me. I'm right next to your room, nice and handy like. And, don't worry. I put the bill on your tab, same as you always want me to do."

"Gentlemen, I will say good night," Beatrix said as she left the lobby. She turned and reminded Horace, "Tomorrow, breakfast and then we must be ready to leave at nine."

"I'm glad you're here," Horace said a second time as he led Fred over to a chair. "I was just telling Doctor Howell we needed your help, and here you are!" He was so excited he shook Fred's hand a second time.

Theo came into the lobby and joined them. "And Horace, just what have you gotten yourself into this time? I heard two stories. One was a bunch of dead crows, which I got to tell you, doesn't make much sense, even for you, even if it has something to do with your granddaughter. And, the other is some mischief about a dead woman with three knives stuck in her back."

"To tell you the truth, both stories are true. Phoebe's more concerned about the crows than anything else. Well, at least she was at the start. But, it's the dead woman that's the real head-scratcher. From what we can figure out, she's been around here for some forty years, but nobody knows much about her. That's about what we have so far. Other than that, all we do know is that she was from somewhere in France and she had a broken toe."

"Broken toe? What's that got to do with her getting murdered?"

"Not much. We went through all the old medical records, and that's all we got, a broken toe. That's all we know for sure about her right now. Lots of rumor and stories, but, well, who knows?. So, I'm saying, that it's a real mystery. That, and she lived out in a small place along the river and cleaned rooms at a few local guest houses."

Fred let out a low whistle, then asked, "Not much to go on, is it? And what's the lady doctor got to do with it? She tagging along with you, or did you invite her?"

"No, Doctor Howell was something of a surprise. Apparently, Phoebe wrote to her about the dead crows, and she came down on her own. I know what you think of her, so let's do our best to work together. She may come across as different, but she's got it where it counts." He pointed to his head. "Anyway, we're getting together for breakfast at 8, and I'd like you to join us."

"Wait a minute. Wait just a minute. Beatrix Howell is here? Horace, are you serious?" his brother asked, and he didn't sound pleased.

"Why? What's wrong?" he asked.

Theo stared at him. "Plenty, since you asked. One minute she is talkative, and then suddenly it's as if she just went into a trance …"

"She's thinking, that's all," Horace shot back.

"Fine. That's what you say. So she's thinking, and when she thinks she ices over, freezes everyone out. And then when she talks, she takes everything literally."

"I don't see the problem. Some people are like that." Horace said firmly.

Theo continued, "Yes, I know You for one. I've known that for years. And the other thing is, have you noticed she only wears blue? Blue dresses, blue blouses, blue skirts. Nothing but blue, all the time. Clarice mixes it up a little, so do Harriet and Phoebe, so does everyone other woman on this planet, but not Beatrix."

"No, come to think of it, I never did notice. You might be right," Horace answered. He paused, then added, "Anyway, I always wear grey. Nearly always, that is."

"That's my point. You two are alike, and sometimes that is downright uncomfortable for the rest of us. One of you is bad enough, but two …"

Horace fought to control his temper, and said very evenly, "Well, Beatrix is here now, and like I said, she's got brains, and that's what matters. That's all that matters, as far as I'm concerned."

"And like I said, you two are alike. Bookends, with plenty of books so you don't get too close to each other," Theo said. "Well, I just hope you keep it that way. Well, I'm dead tired and off to bed."

Fred and Horace watched him trudge up the stairs, holding tightly to the railing. "He's just tired, that's all. Crabby, the way children get when they haven't had their nap. Don't pay him no never-mind, he'll be all right by morning," Fred consoled his employer.

Horace wasn't quite as optimistic.

CHAPTER FIVE

Horace was enjoying his third cup of coffee when Beatrix walked into the hotel restaurant; his fifth by the time Fred sat down, followed almost immediately by Theo and Clarice. "You look quite smart in that blue dress," Theo said.

"I always wear blue. Thank you," Beatrix answered.

"I've been out doing a bit of reconnaissance," Fred announced, quickly changing the subject. "All seems to be quiet. A lot quieter than when we were here in the summer. Nothing further to report, Sir." He waited for a young waitress to fill his coffee cup. "You know, one of the great virtues of this man's country is coffee. As soon as you empty a cup, a waitress is right there to fill it up again. You don't find that in Europe. You take those Frenchies, now they charge you an arm and a leg for a thimble full of it, and it's bitter as anything. Those Romans were the same way, you remember when we were over there a while back?"

Horace noticed that Beatrix remained silent, her head down, waiting for the chatter and small talk to wind down. "Perhaps we should discuss the business at hand," he said. "The murder, remember? I'm sure we've all been turning it over in our minds. Any ideas or thoughts that might be helpful? Beatrix, you first."

"I have already contacted Doctor Landis to let him know of our findings from his ledgers, and that we have put them back where we found them, as well as telling him we put the soiled lab coats in the hamper. I offered to have them cleaned, but he said that was not necessary. I also requested a copy of the pathology report and a sample of Miss LeBeau's hair and any samples from under her fingernails. They may prove helpful."

"I take it you suspect arsenic if you want hair samples," Theo said.

His comment caught her off guard, and momentarily distracted her, then she smiled. "Right now I am keeping an open mind, but I would not rule it out yet," she answered.

"Even with three knives in her back?" Theo asked. From the tone of his voice it was obvious he was not impressed with her answer.

"At some point the authorities will release the body for burial, so, yes. I think having samples would be prudent," she said firmly.

Horace continued, "Fred, you scouted around town. Anything come to mind?"

"Well, like I said, Boss, I scouted around town after you went up to your room last night, just to see what's what, and then again this morning. The place is real quiet. Course, I didn't quite know what I ought to be looking for, so I probably didn't see anything. Soon as we get back from seeing the dead lady's place, I figured I might go over to Dominic's to get a haircut and get these shoes cleaned up a bit. After that, go over to a diner for coffee and a sinker, just to see if there's any intelligence to be gotten hold of. After that, the hardware store."

"That sounds like a reasonable plan," Horace said. "So, aside from Fred scouting around, it's a matter of looking at the scene of the crime." He lifted his half-empty coffee cup in a half-hearted toast to the day's work, "Here's hoping for the best."

Beatrix lifted her cup, adding, "I think much will be revealed today, assuming that the woman's house has not been too badly disturbed. I do not have much confidence that Chief Garrison was scrupulously careful during his investigation. Good luck to us all. We will most certainly need it."

"Our flyboys, Rickenbacker and the rest of them, just before they went on patrol, they always said, 'Good hunting'" Fred announced as he lifted up his cup. "So here's to us and good hunting."

The police chief waved to them from the lobby, then paced the floor as he waited for them to leave their table, eager to take them out to the LeBeau house. "Wasn't expecting all of you," he muttered. "Couple of you'll have to sit in the rumble seat."

"Theo, let's take it! I've never been in a rumble seat before. I hear it's quite the smart thing to do," Clarice said brightly. She untied the scarf from her neck to put over her hair.

"I suspect you may find it to be an over-rated experience," Beatrix cautioned her as Theo helped his wife into the back seat.

They drove through town, across the swing bridge over the Kalamazoo River, and then onto the road that ended at Ox-Bow. Horace remained silent, staring at the water. Even from a distance it had a calming effect. His mind wandered to his *Aurora*. He missed being on his boat, and wished it was here in Saugatuck.

"It's not much of a house," the chief told them as everyone got out of his car. "More like a shack than anything else. Ma used to say some women can't help themselves because they are natural born casual house-keepers, but our victim doesn't even rise to that standard. This place is worse, just so you know."

Clarice stared at the place and whispered to her husband, "Oh, my!" Theo just stared in silence, his mouth open.

"That was something of an understatement, Chief," Horace said quietly as he looked at the house. Paint and a brush had obviously had no connection with the clapboard siding since the turn of the century. The only question was which century. A shutter from the left front window was off and leaning against the house. The chimney was in such desperate need of tuck-pointing he could see light coming through between some of the bricks. Decades earlier there might have been a front lawn, but the weeds had taken over. "Sure is a grim sight," Horace muttered. "You ever need a haunted house at Halloween, here's the place."

"Watch that second step going up to the porch," the chief said. "Couple of the boards are about to give way. When me and Charlie were carrying her out on the stretcher he almost went through the boards, so watch yourselves. Oh, and the porch isn't any too solid, either. I wouldn't do the Charleston on it if I were you." He pushed open the unlocked front door, his shoulder against the wood, the hinges squeaking in protest.

Beatrix followed the chief into the house, inhaling the air, then hurried back to the porch, her eyes closed as she leaned against the building. "You all right?" Horace asked. She ignored him at first, finally nodding she would be okay.

The air was foul and stale, reeking of mould and mildew, garbage that had been aging for at least a few days and probably longer, and the stench of a cat or cats. Far worse was what Doctor Theo sometimes called the "stench of poverty and old age" where the elderly occupants keep the windows closed to avoid a draft. "I suppose after a while they get used to it," he had said years earlier of a similar house.

Above all, the place was cluttered with filth. There were several piles of clothing on chairs, old rags in a corner, and piles of newspapers and magazines throughout the front room. There was no place to sit without shifting the debris. A small table held dirty dishes and the remains of a meal, dried and stuck to the plates. It left all of them staggered in shock, and Clarice quickly pulled off her scarf, bunched it up, and held it in front of her nose and mouth.

"The poor woman, living this way," Clarice said softly to no one in particular. "I'm sorry, I've got to go back outside." She joined Beatrix on the porch.

"A pile for everything," Horace observed through tightened lips.

"And everything in its pile," Theo echoed. Both men looked at each other as they remembered the adage from their grandmother.

The chief was still showing Fred, Horace, and Theo where they had found the body when Beatrix returned. She startled them, not by her presence, but her appearance. She was a completely different woman. The blanched look on her face was replaced with a healthy glow. Her eyes were bright, almost fierce with excitement, shoulders back, and a tight smile on her face. To his surprise, Beatrix looked at Horace and ran her right finger along the side of her nose to let him know she was in her element. He repeated her gesture and added, "The game's afoot!"

"You found the body there," Beatrix told the chief. "Now, the outline was definitely done before you removed the body, and you traced it precisely?"

"That's standard police procedure," he told her. She did not comment that he had not truly answered her question.

She dropped to her knees in the middle of the outline. "Your magnifying glass, please, Sherlock," she asked. Horace smiled and handed her a small folding magnifier, adding, "Irene."

For the next few minutes she remained on her hands and knees, carefully and slowly and thoroughly exploring the floor inside the chalk lines, giving particular attention to the outline of the hands and face. At times, her head was practically on the floor, looking for any clue, turning this way and then another direction, hoping the light would reveal a vital clue. The rest of the group remained silent, not wanting to interrupt her concentration until she was finished. Theo helped her up to her feet and asked, "Well?"

She said nothing, and went back outside. The chief watched her leave, his eyebrows raised at her unusual behavior. "She does that when she's thinking," Clarice said. The chief rolled his eyes, and moved toward a door leading from the parlour into the back of the house.

"Through here is the kitchen. At least it's something less of a mess," the chief said, leading them into the next room.

He was marginally correct. The kitchen was cleaner, but the stench of mould and mildew was just as intense. A small bunch of fennel was rotting on the counter, adding an acrid and sweet smell. The only thing unusual was a door in the wall opposite the sink. Horace tried the knob, but it was locked. "Only door in the place that won't open," Garrison said flatly as Horace pulled on it again. "Locked."

"Wouldn't surprise me if there's a skeleton hiding behind it," Fred muttered. "Can't see any point in spending much time in this pest house, if you were to ask me, which I reckon you're not. Asking, that is."

"You didn't try forcing the door?" Horace asked. The chief ignored him.

"I wouldn't bother opening up the ice box. We looked, and it's pretty rank. I doubt she bought much ice on a regular basis, least ways, not for a while," the chief warned them. "That stuff will have to be thrown out. Should have been by now."

They continued to look around the house, until the chief yawned and asked if they had seen enough, then moved toward the front door. "Who found the body?" Horace asked once they were outside.

"Neighbor lady next door by the name of Meldon. Mary Bertha Meldon. She looks, well, she looked, in on Miss LeBeau from time to time, just to make sure she was all right. Brought her groceries and things like that the last year or so when she didn't get out so much. Postmaster told me she picked up her mail, not that there ever was much for her. Just a letter once in a while, and the Sears catalogue, maybe a few other pieces like that. When she hadn't seen her for a couple of days she came over and rapped on the door. Our victim didn't answer, so she came in and found her on the floor with three knives sticking out of her back."

"Not an easy thing to find," Clarice said softly as she shuddered. "How did she seem to take it? It must have been a horrible shock."

"Alright, I guess. Leastwise she wasn't wailing and crying all over the place by the time we got out here. Just a little shaky, which is natural, I guess," Garrison answered. "Her man must have quieted her down some. Then again, some of these old timers have seen worse than this, so who's to say? Anyway, he's retired so if you want to talk to him he's usually down to the Green Parrot this time of day. Just ask for Jack, and he'll answer right up."

Horace looked over toward Fred and gave him a slight nod. Fred barely nodded his head, understanding that he had an assignment to talk with Mr. Melden.

"And his wife? What does she do?" Beatrix asked.

"Do? I don't think she does much of anything other than being a housewife, you know, cooking and cleaning, things like that. Like I said, I spoke with her after she told us about the victim, over to their place next door. Seemed friendly enough, and helpful. She isn't exactly what you'd call 'house-proud' but she keeps a tight place compared to this one."

"Well, then I would say she works quite hard," Beatrix bristled.

"Well, I guess that is one way of looking at it, if you call cooking and cleaning real work," the chief snorted.

Beatrix was about to reply when Clarice startled her by putting a hand on her arm. "It's not worth it, dear. That sort of man will never understand." Beatrix nodded in agreement.

"Well, we might as well get back to town," the chief said. "I got other things to do than stand around in this shack of a house."

"Are you not going to lock the door?" Beatrix asked. "It is a crime scene."

"Doc, the only crime here is the way she let it get run down. If someone was to put a match to the place I'd think long and hard about arresting them for arson. My guess is the Village Council might give them a medal for cleaning up the place," he snickered.

"Then, I take it you will have no objection if we come back another time, should our inquiries warrant it?" she asked.

"Lady, fill your boots. Like I said, we found out all anyone's going to find out. Now, if I were you, I'd be real sure to wear one of your surgical outfits if you're going to go pawing through her things," the chief laughed. "And better put a mask on while you're at it."

"I do not like that man," Beatrix said firmly when they were back in the lobby of the Butler. "He is quite uneducated and rude. He is a perfect candidate for an alternative use of a rolling pin or frying pan."

"I agree with you! A good hard swat where the pants meet the seat of the chair might help, but there's not much we can do about it," Horace told her before changing the subject. "It seems to me that we're going to need some form of transportation. Fred, you want to see if we can hire a car and driver?"

"A car, yes, but I can't see the point of paying someone to drive you around when you got me and I've been driving you and Doctor Theo around for years. I'll see if I can scare up a car for rent.

Maybe if I go out to the gas station I might have some luck. You got something in mind?"

"You're absolutely right about driving. Just a car, then. Nothing fancy, as long as there's room for all of us," Horace told him. "All we need is something that runs and is reliable. Fred, save yourself some effort and check at the front desk to see if the manager has any ideas where you can get one. That'll save time, because I'd still like you to see what you can learn from this Mister Melden."

"Yes, Sir, Boss," Fred said. He got up and walked over to the check-in desk, and then returned almost immediately.

"This came for you, Doctor Howell," he said as he handed Beatrix an envelope before going back to see the manager again.

The Balfours watched as she opened the envelope and read the contents. She smiled. "Well, this is about what I thought we would learn. It is from Doctor Landis. The pathology report on the blood work found a very high level of arsenic. That is what I suspected when I saw the lines on her fingernails. Now it is confirmed. But, there were also high levels of cobalt, cadmium, mercury and copper acetate. That seems quite odd, considering her circumstances."

"Odd is hardly the word for it. She was a walking chemical factory. How high was the arsenic level?" Theo asked.

"Practically off the charts. The striations on the fingernails indicate she had been ingesting it for a long time, so we can rule it out as an immediate cause of death," Beatrix said. "No, I said that incorrectly. She died of long-term arsenic poisoning."

"That and three knives in her back," Theo answered, with a growl.

"But where would an elderly woman get all of these chemicals?" Beatrix asked. "That does not make sense. Admittedly, we know little about her history, but she would have had to have worked in a factory or machine shop for many years to get to these levels. We have not heard anything about that."

"We don't know anything about her past," Horace reminded her.

Clarice interrupted. "I'll see what I can find out from some of the other women in town. Perhaps they might know." She stood up and walked to the front desk.

"It would have to have been at an industrial factory or a foundry, perhaps one that does metal castings. Another alternative might be a pottery or ceramics factory, but that is far less likely," Doctor Howell suggested.

"Ox-Bow?" Horace asked.

"There is very little chance of that. Besides, Harriet said that she barely knew Miss LeBeau. If she had been at the school, Harriet would have known about it and said something. No, not Ox-Bow. We must ascertain whether or not there is a foundry nearby, or a pottery. A tannery might be a possibility, as well."

The three physicians sat in silence, watching as Clarice came back with a smile on her face. "Well, well, well, this might help. Some of the ladies from town are coming here for a duplicate bridge game in the dining room this afternoon. The clerk said that your granddaughter's teacher, Lila, has to go to a piano recital up in Holland, so there will be room for me."

"Thunderation! You're going to play cards this afternoon? I thought you were going to help with the investigation," Horace chastised her.

"Horace, where there is a group of women playing bridge there is conversation and an exchange of local news. And before you say it, it is news and discussion about the local happenings and not gossip! An exchange of information. Is that clear? So, I *am* helping with the investigation in my own way," she told him firmly.

Horace looked at her, then finally said, "Oh, I understand."

"Good. I'm glad you do. That means there is hope for Theo."

"Clarice, as long as you're talking to some of the ladies, would you see what you can learn about factories and foundries in the area?" Theo asked. She nodded in agreement. He turned back to Beatrix. "Anything else in Landis's letter?"

"I had asked him to look at samples of anything found under her fingernails. Dirt. Nothing else. Just plain old-fashioned garden dirt. No skin from scraping an attacker, nothing. And, that reconfirms what I did not find on the floor of her house. I looked for scratches in the wood. There would normally be evidence of an attack — clawing at the wood floor. There was not. I do not know if she was struck down from behind or not. All I do know is that there is no evidence that she struggled with her attacker." Beatrix handed Horace the letter from Doctor Landis.

He looked at it for a while, trying to make sense of it. Finally, he asked, "So, what are the implications?"

"I am still not certain. The levels of the metals in her blood are alarmingly high and highly unusual under the circumstances as we know them. As for the arsenic, that is a true mystery. It is the result of a very long and continuous history of ingesting it, and confirmed by the hair and fingernail samples. All we know for certain is that she did not take poison to end her life. Nor is it likely that someone forced her to drink it."

"No. No, she was stabbed to death," Theo said softly.

"I am not so certain," Beatrix told him.

"Thunderation!" Horace exploded, "If she didn't die of arsenic poisoning and she didn't die from three knives in her back, what did kill her? What makes you say she wasn't stabbed to death?"

"There wasn't enough blood on the back of her dress. I believe I told you that before. If she had been stabbed, at least one of them should have presented a much larger bloodstain and a widespread splatter. The second should have left a smaller splatter pattern, and less so for the third. There was not enough on her clothing, nor on the floor of her house to indicate she was stabbed to death. I looked to see if the floor had been scrubbed. There was no evidence of blood or cleaning. There is either something wrong here, or we are missing a vital clue."

"What if she was killed elsewhere and well, dropped on the floor of her house so that someone would find her?" Theo asked.

"That," Beatrix said slowly, "is a very interesting question."

"Well, let's hope Clarice learns something that starts answering the questions," Theo replied.

"Say, Doc, when those ladies play cards, do they do it for money? That's gambling you know, and some folks wouldn't say it is right," Fred asked.

"Fred, you'd have to ask Mrs. Balfour, and if I were you, I'd stay out of it."

CHAPTER SIX

After school that afternoon, Harriet and Phoebe drove slowly past the Butler Hotel, hoping they might see Horace or Beatrix. "There's Grandfather!" Phoebe shouted as she pointed to Horace, sitting in a rocking chair on the front porch. Harriet parked her car and they walked over to see him. Horace was so lost in thought that he didn't realize they were standing next to him until Phoebe touched his sleeve. "Grandfather," she said softly.

It startled him, but once he realized who it was, he smiled, "Finally a worthy interruption!"

"Interruption from what?" Harriet asked.

"Trying to solve this mystery. Well, the two mysteries, really. The crows you told me about and Miss LeBeau. No one else thinks I'm right, but I am starting to get the idea they might be connected. It's all a bit foggy now, and I just can't figure out how they fall together."

"You will, Grandfather. You always do!" Phoebe told him.

"Thunderation, girl! You have a lot of faith in an old man. Now, I was just thinking that since we had dinner at your house last night, I ought to return the favour. And, since I don't have the *Aurora* with me, much less Mrs. Gar, let's do it here at the hotel. What do you two say to that?"

"Dinner in a hotel? Really? Please, Mother, can we? I promise to use all of my Paris Manners!" Harriet laughed and agreed, and they settled on six o'clock to meet in the dining room.

As they all came down from their rooms a couple of hours later, , Clarice said, "Alright all of you, we are not talking shop tonight. Dinner is not the place for talking about a murder, especially with Phoebe here. Is that understood? Good heavens, I've had decades of you talking about medicine and surgery every time we get together. I want tonight to be different, so no talk about work. Let's make Harriet and Phoebe feel special."

"I agree with you, Mrs. Balfour," Beatrix said quietly. "A ghastly murder is not a conversation for dinner."

Despite their best attempts to avoid that one topic of conversation, inevitably one of them would ever so easily circle back to Miss LeBeau or the trio of dead crows. Clarice would glare over her glasses at Horace and Theo, putting an end to it, if only for a few minutes. Only Beatrix kept her promise, but, as usual, she hardly said anything throughout the meal. She was either lost in thought or had retreated into her own world.

Clarice was not pleased with them, then for a moment forgot her own instructions about not discussing the topic. "Alright, let me tell you what I think. Horace and Theo, you are making a colossal mistake!" She pushed her left index finger down on the table to emphasize her point.

"What do you mean? Theo asked.

"You are looking at this from just one angle — a medical one. From what you've said, she was stabbed and poisoned, but you don't know what killed her. That's because all you are looking at is the cause of death. You are missing everything else because you are not even looking for it."

Both men looked startled. Even Beatrix looked up, interested in this new approach.

"Remember back in the early days when you were starting out? If you don't I do, because I was there. You had new patients come into your office and I'd get to know them as they registered and while they waited. When it was time for an exam, you got to know them; everything about them. Where they came from, what they did for work and fun, family members, all the rest. You talked to them and their families and anyone else to get more information. Then you started looking at the medical side."

"Thunderation, it's a bit hard to carry on a conversation with a dead woman," Horace retorted. "Especially when she doesn't seem to have a family or even any friends."

"Granted. But think of it this way: She owned that home, or even if she rented it, then someone had to have owned it. That means there are records at the village hall. And, if not there, then somewhere. There has to be a deed, and that means a lawyer who drew up the contract, and that lawyer might have drawn up her will. That lawyer would have a name. And then you talk to him. Have you even thought about looking for a will, much less the attorney? Between that and talking to the neighbors, there's no telling what you might find."

The two brothers looked at each other and then back at Clarice, stunned by her comments. "Well, it seems logical to me," she half-apologized, for a moment thinking she had over-stepped her bounds.

"Please do not think it is necessary to apologize, Clarice. Always hide something in plain sight, right, Sherlock?" Beatrix added, giving him a slight smile.

"Well said, Irene," Horace answered, returning her smile. "And you are absolutely right, Clarice. We've been fixed on the medical side to the exclusion of everything else."

Theo nodded in agreement, and Fred was broadly smiling, almost chortling, as he was planning how he could scout the area and discover some deep, dark secret.

"I still think I should do what I do best," Beatrix said quietly. "I still want to pursue the results of the blood test and see if I can find a cause for the abnormalities."

"What do you have in mind?" Horace asked.

"Since Doctor Landis is the only physician here, I am certain he has been appointed the public health administrator. At least it stands to reason, and there is precedent for it. He may be able to give us some insight into how Miss LeBeau could have ingested so much arsenic and the other metals."

Theo wasn't certain it would be very beneficial, but agreed with his brother that she should continue her line of work. As usual, the brothers had different reasons for agreeing. Theo still found Beatrix difficult, so he was happy she would be out of his way. Horace knew Beatrix was a pathologist and uncomfortable talking with strangers. If Landis or anyone else wasn't forthcoming, Beatrix would keep probing and asking questions until she had answers. She could do more to help by following her own interests than anything else.

"So, it looks like we have a plan, and everyone has a job to do," Horace said as he pushed his chair back from the table. "And, according to my genuine United States Army wristwatch, if we don't dilly-dally, we have time to get over to the soda fountain for some ice crème. My treat!"

"None for us," Clarice said. "I'm watching my figure."

"I'll join you," Theo said to his brother, starting to push back his chair.

"And I am also watching your figure, so I think you can afford to miss dessert tonight, dear," she teased. Theo shook his head. "Count me in."

"All right," Horace agreed. "Harriet and Phoebe, Beatrix, what about you three ladies? And I already know Fred won't turn me down."

"Oh, all right, you can count me in, then," Clarice surrendered with a dramatic sigh. "No telling what mischief you three could get into on your own."

It was only after Harriet agreed, that Beatrix said she would come along. On their walk, Phoebe whispered to Beatrix, "You can have a Green River if you want that instead. Grandfather always has one."

"I will bear that in mind. Thank you," Beatrix gravely answered. "I am not familiar with them, so perhaps I should try one tonight,"

If only for a few minutes, dead crows and murder were forgotten. Fred had his double fudge sundae while all the others had a Green River. "What an interesting color," Beatrix said as she looked at her drink. She held the drink up to the light. "What a beautiful translucent green." She didn't add that the color reminded her of something.

"It tastes better than it looks," Phoebe told her. "You ought to try it before the fizz goes flat."

Beatrix took a sip and winced. "Oh, I do not agree!" was all she said. She slowly sipped at her drink, then took a swallow of water. "I believe it is an acquired taste which I have yet to acquire," she told them.

"Maybe you'll have another one some time," Horace suggested.

"Perhaps not," she answered distantly. She held up the half-emptied glass, wordlessly staring at it.

"What is it? Something wrong?" Horace asked.

"No. No, there is nothing wrong, thank you. There is something about the color. This may sound strange, but it reminds me of something. It will come to me. Thank you for the dinner and dessert. I must go for a walk." Beatrix got up and left the drugstore.

"That, my elderly brother, is a perfect example of why she sends shivers down my spine. She's quirky and inconsistent," Theo said quietly.

"She's thinking about something, a clue, maybe. She walks when she thinks," Horace told him. "I admire her brain-power, even if you don't."

"Right. All I'm saying is just watch your back."

A few minutes after Beatrix left, the young man behind the soda fountain started cleaning up, making it obvious that he was ready to go home for the night. Harriet also was eager to get home and get Phoebe to bed. As usual, it was left to Clarice to notice all of this, and suggested that it was time for them to leave. They stood outside on Butler Street for a few minutes, talking and saying good night, before going their own ways.

"Think I'll go down to the Big Pavilion and snoop around a bit," Fred said. "Most of the tourists are gone, but maybe I'll scare up some intelligence from the locals. See you in the morning." Horace, Theo, and Clarice watched as he loped off.

"Well, just the three of us," Horace said. "Say, Clarice, you never had a chance to tell us what you learned at the bridge game."

"You're not going to like it, but not a thing. Everyone knew Miss LeBeau had died, of course, and they all claimed they knew about her, but no one knows a thing. Some of them can't even remember the last time they saw her. I had the feeling they were sincere and not just hiding something. So, I didn't learn a thing. And nothing about foundries or factories around here that might be the reason for arsenic," Clarice said as she walked between the two men.

"You think they were holding out on you? You know, a conspiracy of silence?" Theo asked, probing again.

"I doubt it. They seemed genuine about it. In fact, they took up a collection to help pay for her burial," Clarice sighed. "That is just so sad. No money for a proper burial."

"Any idea when the service is?" Horace asked.

"Just as soon as the chief releases the body, and that probably depends on you three. A couple of men at Koening's were conscripted to make a coffin, and the Methodist preacher is going to do the graveside service. I doubt there will be any reception. I heard one of the women say that they ought to go, just so someone from town will be there."

The three of them walked in silence, thinking about the sad ending of Miss LeBeau's life. "I think we ought to go," Horace said softly.

"You getting a little sentimental in your old age, or just afraid no one will come to your burial?" Theo asked icily, still disquieted by Beatrix's abrupt departure.

"Perhaps," Horace said quietly. "It might be interesting to see who else might turn up."

"You mean the killer?" Clarice asked.

"The killer might find it irresistible," Horace said.

"Interesting," Theo observed. "Let's be sure to find out when the service will be."

The next morning, Horace said, "Fred, why don't you drive Doctor Howell over to see Doctor Landis …"

"There is no reason for that. I am perfectly comfortable walking," Beatrix objected.

"Yes, of course you are." Horace continued. "Fred can drop you off and wait for you. If Landis isn't there, then he can bring you back here. We've got a few other threads to follow," Horace told her.

"Yes, I understand. I apologize for interrupting you."

"While they're doing that, Theo, what about you talking to some of the merchants, maybe the manager at the bank, and see what you can learn? I can go over to City Hall and see if we can find out anything about the property. Now, Fred, if you leave Doctor Howell with Doctor Landis, go have coffee and see if you can find out anything. Let's all try to get back to the hotel around noon to compare notes. Clarice should be back from calling on Mrs. Heath."

Beatrix interrupted. "That is very good to know. From what I heard this summer, she has wonderful connections with everyone in town.

"In that case, none better. Let's not forget we still need to talk to that fellow McGuffy," Horace continued.

"McGuffy isn't the right name, I don't think," Fred said. "Didn't he write those books for children? Melden, isn't it? Yeah, I'm sure. Melden."

"Well, we still want to talk with him and his wife," Horace said. "They lived right next door, so if anyone knows anything about this mysterious woman, they're our best hope. Let's go to work and solve this because we still have to figure out what killed the murder of crows."

"What murder of what crows?" Fred asked. "I thought I came down for real murder."

Beatrix glared at Horace. "Must you? You are incorrigible. Please, do not even start that again. The double entendre of a pun is a very low form of humor."

Horace whispered to Fred, "I'll explain later. Right now, I'll get over to the city hall and see what we can find."

"To be correct, it is a village hall. Saugatuck is a village, not a city," Beatrix pointed out.

"Right. Then I'll get over to the village hall," Horace said. "Doctor Howell, good luck, good hunting, and we'll see you back here in a few hours."

The noon fire whistle was just starting to blow when Beatrix hurried up the front steps of the Butler Hotel to join Horace and Fred on the veranda. "I hope you have some good news," Horace said wearily as he stood up to greet her. He had to tap Fred on his shoulders to remind him to stand up, and tap him again to remind him to remove his hat.

"Why? What did you learn?" she asked. "Please tell me that they have property records."

"They do. And all they had was a legal description of the property, and that it was an improved lot, which means it had a building on it, probably the house, and that it was a cash sale. No mortgage, no bank, no lawyer. Just a simple cash transaction for five hundred sixty dollars," Horace answered.

"What about the previous owner? Surely there must have been something?" Beatrix asked.

"Just a name, and no one remembered the seller."

"We done did strike out faster than ol' Babe Ruth himself," Fred added. "I didn't do much better, either."

"Anyway, that took half an hour or so, and then we went over to the newspaper office. I'd read somewhere that papers keep a morgue," Horace began.

"I gotta tell you, Doctor Howell, it weren't no morgue like I've seen. No bodies, just big files of paper," Fred chimed in.

"Fred's right: A newspaper morgue is where they keep records of people so that when they die they can write the obituary in time for their deadline. Anyway, the Commercial Record has one. By the way, all of us — you, Fred, Theo and Clarice, and I are in it thanks to our adventure last summer. I thought you'd like to know that. But when it came to Miss LeBeau — nothing. The editor was hoping I'd have something to add, which I didn't. From the looks of it, like Clarice said late last night, they'll bury her in the Potters Field at the cemetery, and that's about it."

The three of them sat in silence, until Fred finally asked, "What about you, Doctor Howell?"

Beatrix looked away from them, out towards the water, "It was as unpleasant as it is unproductive."

"What do you mean?" Horace asked, confused.

"As you know, my intent was to shed some light on the high arsenic and metals levels in her blood report. Doctor Landis suggested that it might be a result of drinking the water from the river. I asked how that would be possible, and he explained that there are a number of paper mills and manufacturing plants further up the Kalamazoo River which discharge their waste water into the river. There are, apparently, very high levels of toxins contaminating the river. He attributes her blood levels to that.

"I questioned whether simply drinking water from the river could be the cause for it, and he shrugged his shoulders and said, 'perhaps.'"

"However, when we were at Miss LeBeau's house, you will remember that she had a faucet and not a hand pump in her kitchen, which leads me to believe that her water comes from the city, and not directly from the river. I am quite sure there is a purification system, but we should verify this."

"Good work," Horace said, "but that doesn't seem unpleasant."

"Unfortunately, I asked why, as the public health official for both Saugatuck and Douglas, he had done nothing to remediate the polluted river water. He told me that it was not in his best interests, and he had no desire to fight a battle with the mill owners upriver. I am afraid I was sharp with him, and reminded him it was a physician's duty .

"He rather heatedly warned me against meddling. As I could see no favorable outcome to our conversation, I thanked him for his time and left. As I said a few moments ago, it was neither productive nor pleasant."

Horace ran his right hand through his hair. "Probably didn't want to upset the apple cart and drive patients away. I suppose in a way, it's understandable."

"It may be understandable, but I do not approve of it."

Lunch was not jovial. In addition to the three of them having learned nothing that morning, Theo added that a few shop owners remembered her working for them part time, but it had been years earlier and their memories had faded She was honest, a steady worker, but never talked much, and certainly not about herself. As for the manager of Fruit Growers' Bank, he confidentially whispered that he wasn't acquainted with the late Miss LeBeau.

"Well, Clarice, it's up to you to rescue us," Horace said.

"Sorry. Nothing, I called on Mrs. Heath and several more of the ladies from the village, and they said only that they had heard her name, but never made her acquaintance. She was not what Mrs. Heath called 'a joiner' or very community minded in any organization, church, or committee. In a word, nothing," Clarice told them.

"Not even any gossip?" Fred asked.

"These women are not the type to gossip. At most, they exchange news and share commentary and speculation," Clarice told him flatly. "From the tone of their voices, I do not think they held her lack of civic-mindedness in very high esteem. All of them agreed with that statement."

Only Beatrix saw the humor in her comment, and looked down at her plate to hide her thin smile. She became serious again and said. "The arsenic was ingested over at least a year, perhaps more, maybe as long as a decade. Perhaps someone had a grudge and wanted to make her suffer. Or, perhaps it was a sadistic act of slow torture. Such might well have been her fate. And, truly, it would have been a horrible way to die, in stages, like that."

"But who?" Horace asked. "The only people who had any contact with her were the Meldens. That doesn't make sense. It couldn't be for the property and house. We all saw what that looked like."

"Don't let your imagination run away with you," Clarice cautioned. "It could be anyone. Before long you'll be suspecting the grocer, or perhaps the postmaster. They could have poisoned her food or put something in her mail. The next thing you know, you'll be suspecting the women in town of murdering her because she didn't join anything."

Beatrix looked up slowly and softly said. "Small villages can be hotbeds of people waiting years, a generation or more, for revenge."

CHAPTER SEVEN

As they stood outside the Butler, waiting for Fred to bring up the car, Horace glumly said, "Well, looks like we have two final chances. We either get a nibble this afternoon, or it's time to pull in our lines and go home."

Beatrix looked at Clarice, puzzled. "It's a fishing metaphor. We either learn something this afternoon or we might as well give up and let the chief declare it murder by assailant or assailants unknown," Clarice told her.

"That would not be good," Beatrix whispered. "We must do something!"

"Definitely not good. Let's hope we get something from either the house or the Meldens."

"How shall we handle this?" Theo asked when Fred pulled into the gravel driveway at Miss LeBeau's house.

"Well, it looks like the Meldens are home next door, and since you and Clarice are better with people than the rest of us, that looks like the best place for you two. Fred, you're best at scouting, so what do you say to going along the river, say a hundred yards in each direction, and look for anything out of the ordinary: Foot path, a place where someone ties up for a while, maybe camps out, trash, that sort of thing, anything."

"Nothing I'd like better. It kinda sorta reminds me of that time our unit was along the Meuse over there in France and the captain was worried about how the Huns were maybe trying to sneak around behind us. They were always trying to get the jump on us like that. He sent me out with a couple of fellows and we went upstream a few hundred yards. We could see a track where they were coming down their side, and sure enough, they'd waded through the water and come up about a hundred yards or so on our flank. Well, let me tell you, we put a stop to that in a hurry! I'll see what I can find this time."

"Thank you, Fred. Go do some more scouting," Horace said. "Beatrix, let's see what we can find inside Chateau LeBeau." They watched as Theo and Clarice walked next door and knocked on the Melden's front door.

"Does he always talk about the war?" Beatrix asked.

"Not exactly always, just a lot," Horace told her. "He's a good man."

"Yeah, some of the fellows down to the Green Parrot told me about how Chief Garrison roped you into figuring out how Catherine, that is, Miss LeBeau, died," Mr. Melden said as he invited Clarice and Theo to sit on the porch swing. "I figured you'd want to talk to us. Now, if you ask me, it looked pretty straight forward to me when I found her. Three knives stuck up to the hilt ought to be clear enough even to the chief." He chuckled nervously. "Sure was to me."

Mrs. Melden had come to the door with her husband, then excused herself to put on some water for tea. She returned several minutes later with four cups and saucers on a tray and set them down on a small table in front of them. She seemed nervous, and soon realized she had forgotten the teapot. When she returned, her face was flushed. Clarice wondered if it was from embarrassment or something else.

"I think the real question is who did it," Theo answered his host. "As it turned out, my brother had come down to see his granddaughter, when he first learned of it. And then, well, maybe you know how it is when you're retired and wanting something to keep you busy, so Mrs. Balfour and I came down, too."

"Oh, so that's how it is," Mr. Melden said, perhaps not quite believing their story.

"Well, I am just plain curious. My husband was a doctor for years, and they're such a curious bunch. I think I got it from both of them," Clarice fibbed ever so slightly. "You two living next door to her, you must have known her better than anyone. Sort of makes me curious if you have any thoughts on how she was killed, or who would have wanted her dead." She paused to give them time to answer as she picked up a tea cup to read the manufacturer's name on the bottom of the saucer, smiled, and put the cup back on it. Mrs. Melden took that as a sign it was time to pour.

"I see," Mr. Melden replied. "Yeah, we lived next door and when she was getting up there a bit I'd bring her her groceries, things like that. Not that she ever bought much. Oh, and I can tell you, she liked her liquorice. The wife here looked in on her from time to time. But mostly she kept to herself. We're not the type to pry or interfere, you know. We're willing to help someone out, but we don't like to pry."

"About the only thing we know about her is that years ago she came over from France," Theo said. "That's why we were hoping to find out more about her, or where she lived or anything so we can at least let the family know about her passing."

"Not much help there, either. You're right about coming from France. You could tell by the accent. I thought maybe she was from Quebec, up there in Canada, but she set me straight on that one! A couple of times she mentioned some little place out in the country over near Paris, but she never mentioned nothing about a family. Of course, I never asked much, either. I don't like to pry," Mr. Melden said, repeating himself.

"Kind of sad, in a way. Coming over by herself and living alone and no family. Makes you wonder if she had a past and was trying to hide out over here," Theo suggested.

Mrs. Melden snorted, "Can't imagine her being the type to have a past, as you called it. She once said she was a chambermaid at a little hotel over there where she grew up. Makes you sort of wonder how she scraped together the money just to get over here. Not that I ever asked. Just goes to show you that where there's a will, there's a way." She jumped up again, went into the house, and returned with some stale ginger snaps.

"I was just admiring your china. *Limoges*. It's lovely," Clarice gushed. "You are so fortunate to have it. I'm envious."

"It is pretty, isn't it? It was Mother's and she left it to me."

"That would make any sister jealous," she smiled, carefully watching the woman's face. Instead, their hostess quickly said, "Do try the cookies. I just made them before lunch." Theo was no gourmet, but the cookies were so stale he wondered which week's lunch she meant.

"Dr. Balfour was just telling your husband that we were hoping to find out some information about Miss LeBeau. What concerns me is that so far I don't think anyone has told her family. Apparently, she kept very much to herself. I hope we can at least let them know that she passed away ..." Clarice's voice trailed off, and she looked expectantly at her host. She hoped asking the question a second time would get them talking more freely. "Your cookies are delicious."

"I don't know very much, not really. Practically nothing at all," Mrs. Melden said quietly.

"My thought was that since she was from France, if we knew where she was born, or even where she worked as a chambermaid, that might help. My brother-in-law suggested if we could find out that much, we could write to the parish priest and perhaps he could be of some help."

Their host snorted in derision. "Good luck if it's Paris!"

"Well, it isn't much, but she mentioned someplace called Auvere-sur-Oise, but I have no idea where it is, or whether it's a village or a neighborhood in Paris, or maybe the name of a street," Mrs. Melden said thoughtfully and slowly. "But that was years ago, so maybe I'm mistaken or confused."

"And it might not even exist anymore after the war. A lot of those little hamlets along the front got hit pretty hard and blown to smithereens. Wouldn't surprise me if they're gone for good. Doesn't seem very hopeful. More like a waste of your time," her husband added.

"You might be right," Theo said. "Still, it is worth a try. ... Maybe my brother and Doctor Howell will find some old letters or something in her house. Were you in the war?"

"Me, no. Too old for that one. I was with MacArthur in the Philippines right after we beat the Spanish, then I got the malaria, and the Army sent me home."

"I wish them well," Mrs. Melden said. "Catherine was rather careless the past few years about the house. She never let anyone come in the door, well, unless it was one of us. She sort of let the house go. And, herself, come to think of it if you want the truth of the matter. You could tell she was once a real looker, but I think she sort of gave up. You know how it happens to some people. They just don't care what they look like anymore.

"I don't know what's going to happen to her place. It's really not much of a house to begin with, and it's one good blizzard away from collapsing. The roof, the walls, the floors all sag. And no one will ever get the smell out of there. It's such a pity," their hostess said quietly.

The four of them sat in awkward silence for a few more minutes. "Maybe we ought to be on our way and let these good folks get back to what they were doing," Theo suggested. He stood up, holding out his hand to help Clarice.

"Well, what do you think?" Clarice whispered as soon as they were out the front gate and on the street. She quickly glanced over her shoulder to make sure they were out of earshot.

"I'm not certain," Theo answered. "But I do think they know at least a little more, maybe a whole lot more, than what they told us. Maybe they're being cautious because we're strangers."

"I think they know a *lot* more than what they told us," Clarice said, almost smugly. "Especially Mrs. Melden. She was too flighty. And, both of them seem on edge, nervous. Did you see her jump when we told her that Horace and Beatrix are looking through the house? I think there's something in there!"

"Well, keep it to yourself until we get back to the hotel later on. Horace and Beatrix won't take to being interrupted. Leastwise, she won't," Theo growled.

"You still don't like her; I can tell. So let me tell you something, and for your own good, so you'd better listen. Your brother is just bull-headed enough he might start getting serious about her if you keep fussing so much. You'll push him right into it if you're not careful. So unless you want Beatrix as your sister-in-law, be nice to her, is that clear?"

Theo knew when he had been chastised, and said quietly, "Abundantly clear." He paused to let her words register in his mind, then asked, "What about you? What do you really think of her?"

Clarice shrugged. "She's definitely different but charming in her own way, and she has taken care of herself. Theo, she has a kind heart and a brilliant mind, and if Horace is comfortable with her around, then it's his business, not ours."

'Not our business?' Theo thought to himself. "Every Thursday Clarice invited him to dinner, every holiday, every celebration, she would be with him." The thought made him shudder.

Theo and Clarice found Horace sitting on the front steps of Miss LeBeau's house. "What's wrong, big brother? Did your girlfriend kick you out?" Theo teased. Clarice glared at her husband. He had learned nothing.

"Not exactly. She's looking for evidence and needs to be alone," he answered flatly. "Any sign of Fred yet?"

Theo joined him on the steps for a second or two, until he felt the boards beginning to sag under them. Both brothers got up quickly before the wood crumbled, laughing at their near brush with disaster. "I haven't seen you move that fast since that family of skunks came to the picnic a few years ago!" Clarice howled with laughter.

"We haven't seen him, and that might be good news. With a bit of luck he ran across someone who likes to talk, and maybe he's pumping him for information," Theo said after he regained his composure.

"Thunderation!" Horace answered in disgust. "More likely he's run into some old Doughboy and they're telling each other how they each single-handedly won the war. I'd like him to get back here and pick the lock on that door in the kitchen so we can find out where it goes." He pulled out his pipe, filled it, and lit it before asking, "What did you two find out?"

"Not much. The Meldens were hospitable enough, but if they know anything, they're keeping it close to the chest, and I think they know plenty! Maybe they want to make sure we're on the up and up. Clarice was rather taken with the tea cups. Oh, and they mentioned the name of some place in France where the victim may have lived. I forget, but Clarice will remember the name."

"Well, you made some progress, maybe." Horace blew three quick rings of smoke before barking, "Thunderation. I wish those two would get a move on. I'm sitting in the waiting room again!"

"Patience, Horace. It might be worth it. Beatrix's got a good mind and eye. Let her do her work," his brother said. "You have to admire someone who can stay focused like that and forget everyone and everything else." He turned to Clarice and asked, "What did they say was the name of that town she was from?"

"Auvere-sur-Oise. Apparently it's not too far from Paris," she answered. "From what they said, a lot of those towns were badly damaged during the war, but the Germans never got that close did they?"

"Close enough to shell it to smithereens and back if they wanted to," Theo answered.

"Still, it's better than nothing," Horace said. "While we're waiting, maybe we ought to take a look-see around out in back."

"Better than standing here waiting for the house to come down on itself," Theo agreed. "I'll bet the old girl wasn't any better as a gardener than she was keeping house."

They were just about to go around the corner of the house when Beatrix bolted out the front door and shrieked, "Stop! Stop! Do not take another step! Stop where you are!"

Both men halted, looking toward her.

"Back out of there very slowly and very carefully. Do not touch anything. Just back out carefully, and for heaven's sake, do not stumble around!"

The two men did as she told them, confused as to her alarm.

"What's wrong?" Horace asked. "Nothing but a lot of Queen Anne's Lace back there."

"Thank goodness you didn't go there. That is not Queen Anne's Lace. That is flowering hemlock. Every part of that plant is deadly."

"Looks like some tall weeds with white flowers," Theo said.

"It is deadly flowering hemlock. Everything about it is poisonous, " She repeated. "Flowers, leaves, stalk. I am not certain of the roots, however. All of it is deadly. There's more of it out in back, and it is all infested with nightshade vines and wormwood."

"What?" Horace and Theo asked in unison.

"Whether it is intentionally planted or not, the grounds are covered with poisonous plants." She hurried down the steps and stood in front of them. "Horace, tell me you did not brush up against anything." She was obviously shaken and worried.

"No, we didn't get that far. Neither of us."

Beatrix shocked the brothers and Clarice, by reaching out and taking both of Horace's hands turning them over to look closely at them. "Good. No sign of pollen." Then she turned to Theo and looked at his hands. "Slowly turn around -- you first, Theo. I am looking for pollen on your sleeves and trousers."

She looked their clothes over carefully. "Now, if you start feeling strange, you must let me know."

"Strange could be my brother's middle name," Theo quipped, trying to make light of the situation. He was met with a fierce glare from Beatrix.

"Thank you," was all an ashen-faced Horace could say. "Why would Miss LeBeau allow those plants to grow?" he asked no one in particular.

"Well, that answered our questions about her gardening," Theo said.

They waited only a few minutes more before Fred returned with the car. "Anything to report, Sergeant?" Horace asked.

Fred sat a bit straighter to make his report, almost at attention, but not quite. "Maybe. Right now, I'm happy to report it's all quiet along the shore. I hiked about two hundred yards in both directions and didn't see anything out of the ordinary. But then when I came back, and maybe it was on account of the fact that the light was a bit different, I could see where someone had pulled up in front of the place in a small boat, probably a row boat, and tied it up to a shrub," he answered from behind the wheel.

"What in particular?" Horace asked.

"Just a little v-shaped depression in the sand and the first couple of feet in from the water. Maybe from not too long ago, and definitely a light-weight boat."

"Foot prints? A trail leading up to the house? Anything more?" Theo asked.

"Couldn't see anything more than that, leastwise not a regular path. Might be nothing more than someone out for a row on the river, or doing a bit of fishing. No sign of them having a picnic or nothing like that. If they cleaned their fish, the vermin picked it clean. It's all that I could find."

"Well, you're the expert. We'll keep an eye on the spot and see if anyone else comes calling," Horace said. "Look, before we leave, would you go inside and pick the lock on a kitchen door? Doctor Howell thinks there might be something interesting behind it."

"A kitchen lock? That's child's play," Fred chuckled. "I thought the chief said it didn't go anywhere?"

"Yes, that's what the chief said. Let's be sure he knows what he is talking about," Horace said.

"Want me to teach you lock-picking, Doc?" Fred asked Beatrix as they went into the kitchen.

"No thank you. I do not believe it is a skill I need," she answered, stiffening a little.

Fred looked at the lock for a few seconds, pulled out a set of three skeleton keys, and chose one. He explained, "There are only three different keys for these locks. One of these is the right one." His second choice turned the lock with a screech and groan. "Well, shall we see what's behind here?" he asked.

Beatrix nodded for him to proceed, stepping back and to the side, wondering why Fred had a set of keys with him.

"Well, that got us nowhere," Beatrix said, looking at the open door with a solid wall on the other side. "Fred, please ask the Balfours to join us."

All five of them stared at the door that opened up onto a solid wall. "Thunderation!" Horace snarled. "Who'd be crazy enough to do that?"

"All things considered, I think we know the answer to that one. That woman must have been a real lulu," his brother chuckled. "This just gets more and more interesting. A poisoned victim with three knives stuck in her back, a garden fit for a village poisoner, and a locked door that opens onto a wall. Well, where does that leave us?"

"I believe," Clarice said firmly, "our first duty is to see Chief Garrison and report the garden. It is very dangerous, and considering that people are curious about murder, it is fortunate no one has been going into that patch of hemlock. I am worried about children getting in there. It would kill a youngster."

"And, the nightshade vines," Beatrix added.

"All the more reason to report it," Clarice said. "You can explore the door later, boys. And, you too, Beatrix. We need to report the plants."

"Night shade is not nearly as dangerous. Green peppers, cucumbers, and tomatoes are all members of the same family," Beatrix said.

"And to think Mother always made me eat my vegetables," Fred sighed. "I knew they weren't good for a man. That's why I stick to meat and potatoes."

"Potatoes are from the same family," Beatrix said flatly. Fred chose to ignore her.

On the drive into town Clarice and Theo told Fred and Beatrix what they had learned. No one noticed Beatrix suddenly turning to stare out the window, silently thinking through their discoveries, trying to make sense of it, or at least find some connections. Horace had told her in the past that murder always makes sense, if only to the killer. All she had to do was unravel the knotty chaos and it would make sense to her, as well.

CHAPTER EIGHT

"Well, that just about solves half of this mystery, now doesn't it? You tell me she's got poisoned plants all around her place? That's good to hear, real good. You ask me, she probably got into own garden, maybe fell down, tripped over something, maybe, and that's what did her in! All we have to do is figure out the reason for these knives in her back," the chief said smugly.

"No. I regret having to correct you, Police Chief Garrison, but you are completely wrong," Beatrix said firmly, her eyes flashing with fury at his simplistic answer. "The victim's blood had a high concentration of arsenic. Hemlock, wormwood, and nightshade are plants, organic poisons.. Arsenic is a metal, an element. It is completely different from the others. Furthermore, the plants are not poisoned but poisonous. There is a considerable difference."

"Oh, I see what you're driving at. Different poison, huh?" he hesitantly replied, not really understanding what Doctor Howell was telling him. "Then, I guess you still have your work cut out for you."

"No, I think you have your work cut out for you, getting rid of those poisonous plants," Doctor Horace told him. "Or, at least securing the perimeter before someone goes snooping around and gets killed. Children, maybe. Curious children. I'm sure you don't want that to happen. Undoubtedly there would be an inquest and you would be blamed."

"No, of course not, but why me? Why me?" the chief asked.

"Because it is your crime scene. You took control of the house and property, so that makes it your responsibility," Theo's wife said.

"Yeah? And just how are you proposing I do that?" The chief shot back at them. "I don't want anything to do with a bunch of poison plants. Not even if it was just plain old poison ivy."

"Oh, I assure you, this is nothing like poison ivy," Beatrix said brightly. "Poison ivy will create a miserable rash, but hemlock is lethal. Just a little will kill you. Without exaggeration, there is enough of it at her place to poison the entire village, with sufficient plants left over for all of Douglas."

"Oh, thanks a lot, Doc," the chief answered sarcastically. "You got any ideas how to do it?"

"Well, now, if it was up to me, which it isn't on account of the fact that you're the chief and I'm not, I'd go up to that there armoury in Holland and borrow one of their flamethrowers like we used on the Hun back during the war. Just light that thing up and burn 'em out of there!" Fred interrupted. "That should do the trick."

"And likely burn down just about everything else on that side of the river," the chief said, rolling his eyes. "Any other ideas? Practical ones, maybe?"

"I would suggest you talk with some of the local farmers," Theo said quietly and calmly. "Those boys have experience with noxious weeds. The older ones, especially. And, since there is hemlock out there, maybe they've seen it on their farms, as well. They'd be the best starting place. If they can't handle it, then maybe they know someone who can. Simple as that. In the meantime, you might want to send someone out to post the property and keep trespassers away. Maybe some signs with a skull and bones on it, as well."

"Now you're talking! That sounds a lot more like it. Now, listen, do me a favor. I'll go over to the feed store to talk to someone there about getting rid of the stuff, while you go out and put up the signs and post the land. I got some no trespassing signs in the supply closet, and take along some rope to tie it off, as well," the chief commanded.

"Yes! Yes, we can do that!" Beatrix startled everyone with her enthusiastic answer. "Fred, you will drive Doctor Balfour and me out there right now!" Yet, even before she made for the door the look of energy drained off her face, and she was quiet again. Horace saw her stare into the distance.

On the drive back to the other side of the river, Horace started laughing. Fred looked at him from the rear view mirror; Beatrix turned in his direction and asked what he was thinking.

"Well, all of this talk about poison reminded me, and this is from years ago, when Theo and I were just about to go out to pick wild mushrooms. Mother found out about it, and came running after us, telling us to leave the mushrooms alone because some were poisonous."

Beatrix slowly nodded her head. "And this memory made you laugh?"

"Well, not that part. We weren't happy about not getting some mushrooms so we asked Papa if we could do it. He sided with Mother and said we were to leave them alone and let them grow where they would have morel support!" Horace burst out laughing again.

Beatrix stared at him, her lips tightened. "Morel support?" she asked. "Horace, that is a worse pun that the murder of a murder of crows. Please stay focused."

"Well, I thought it was rather clever."

She gave him a withering look.

It took only a few minutes to rope off the front of the property, then tack the no trespassing signs to a couple of trees. "I think that kitchen door warrants some further study," Beatrix told Horace and Fred. "That's why I wanted to come back out here before the chief decided to join us." She started walking toward the porch.

"She's on to something," Fred whispered to his boss. Horace silently nodded in agreement.

"Horace, I assume you have your pipe with you," Beatrix said. "May I borrow it, please? And your tobacco pouch and matches?" The two men watched as she expertly filled his pipe, tamped down the tobacco, and stood in the kitchen doorway, facing the wall. She lit it, and took several long drags to make certain it would keep burning.

Fred and Horace stood behind her as she held the pipe by its stem, slowly running the bowl along the wall where it met the doorframe. At each corner she paused to puff on the pipe, then resumed her unique exploration. When she finished investigating the two sides and top, she turned around and said, "They are air tight." She dropped to her knees and began checking the line where the wall met the floor. "Also air tight," she told them, ignoring Horace's offer of a hand as she got back to her feet.

"Which tells us … ?" Horace asked.

"Which means we can eliminate the locked door hiding a secret passage. The floor is solid, which means there is not a hidden door leading to a basement room or passage wall. The wall is also solid. In short, there is nothing here."

"But why a locked door that opens to a wall?" Horace asked.

"That may be something we will never know, although it may have been nothing more than a matter of convenience," Beatrix said. "I'm beginning to think the woman was certifiably insane."

"Convenience," Horace asserted. "This door was here in the past, then someone decided to plaster over the parlor room wall, and saved a few bucks by leaving the door on the kitchen side. My guess is that Miss LeBeau didn't do it. Someone before her, probably."

Beatrix ignored their conversation and asked bluntly, "What's on the other side of the wall?"

"That big wardrobe out in the front room," Fred answered.

"Well, since we haven't looked too much in the front parlour, that might be a good place to start," Horace said.

"Brilliant deduction, as always, Sherlock," Beatrix teased.

"Always look in the obvious places, Irene," he teased back.

They tried the handle on the wardrobe and found it locked. "Fred, time for you to work your magic again," Horace said as he moved to one side.

Fred smiled in pure glee, glanced at the loc, and pulled a small leather pouch filled with metal picks from his jacket pocket. "One of them should do it," he told them.

"Those are burglars' tools!" Beatrix gasped.

"No, Ma'am, they're not. Carrying them would be strictly against the law. A man could get sent up the river for carrying burglar tools. This here is a package of genuine dental picks. A dentist down to Chicago, a Doctor Lewis Runyan, real prince of a fellow, sold them to me a year or so back when he'd bought some new ones. 'Fred,' he said to me, 'you never know when you might be able to help someone out if they're in a jam.' Course, now we all know they can be used for other things in a pinch too, like what I'm doing to get this wardrobe opened," Fred smiled as he knelt in front of the door.

He selected two and began working on the lock. "I believe this is very illegal!" Beatrix protested again. The two of them ignored her.

Fred quickly got the lock to open. "There she goes. As easy as opening up old King Tut's tomb. Want to see what's inside?"

"That's the general idea," Horace said, as Beatrix fussed a final time that she did not approve of his methods.

Fred pulled open the right door, then moved the latch on the left, opening up the cabinet.

The three of them were stunned. "Thunderation! What the blazes is all this?"

"Whatever you do, do not touch anything!" Beatrix barely whispered. "We should go outside very quietly and quickly."

"You think it's booby-trapped?" Fred asked in alarm. "I didn't hear any ticking." They didn't debate the point. The three of them hustled out of the house and stood on the porch, peering back into the front room.

"Maybe we should move out to the road," Beatrix proposed. She led them out to the street, and they stood on the opposite side of the car.

"Well, if she booby-trapped that wardrobe, she wouldn't want to blow up the whole house, would she?" Fred asked.

"You assume she knows enough about explosives not to do that," Horace told him.

"And you also assume that she was in the right frame of mind. We can not take any chances with a woman like that," Beatrix added. "It is far more probable that some of the chemicals are unstable, and if the jars are leaking, the fumes would have been trapped in the locked cabinet. We did not want to inhale them."

All three of them stared at the house. "What all is in there?" Horace wanted to know.

"I did not have time to examine it, but it appears to be an array of chemicals, any of which is potentially highly unstable, as I just said. Some of them are likely quite flammable, and from a glance at the labels, all potentially deadly," Beatrix said quietly. "I only got a glance."

"Yeah, well I know a still when I see one, and I definitely saw the smallest still I ever saw on the bottom shelf. You figure she was a bootlegger?" Fred asked.

"That would be highly unlikely considering the size of it, and then we must take into consideration all of the other chemicals," Beatrix replied.

"Maybe she was a chemist before she came here," Horace quipped.

"I seriously doubt it. Remember, we have already learned she was a chambermaid at a small hotel. There is little chance she later became a chemist. If anything, I believe she may have been dabbling in alchemy," Beatrix answered. "Please, I am trying to find the pattern." She walked away from them, pacing up and down the road.

After a long ten minutes Horace looked at his watch, restless, and eager to do something. "I figure it's safe to go back in and have a look."

"Just do not touch anything, please. You must understand, until we know what is in there, that wardrobe is a death trap. And please don't move anything. I can't find the pattern yet," Beatrix told them, as she tapped the side of her head.

"Understood," Horace said grimly, although he doubted there was a pattern to be found.

"Hey, Boss, what's alchemy?" Fred asked.

"It's someone who tries turning lead into gold," Horace answered.

Fred shook his head. "That old girl was nutty as they come if she was trying that."

Beatrix stood silently in front of the wardrobe, looking at the bottles on the shelves. "A very interesting collection of acids on the top shelf. I can assure you, she has no real knowledge of chemistry. The placement is too dangerous. Acids belong on the bottom shelf, always, in case they leak or a bottle falls, especially the strong acids such as we see here. And various minerals and metals on the next shelf. Notice our old friends arsenic, cyanide, and strychnine. Now, this is interesting: a bottle that does not belong here — prosodic SP acid. Now, that is an interesting poison. It is fairly weak and smells of almonds. I would advise you, should you smell it on food or in drink, not to touch it. Someone is possibly trying to poison you. Sweet smelling, but lethal."

Horace smiled, reminded of chemistry lectures at medical school. "I'll keep that in mind," he told her.

"Now, this is curious," Beatrix said as she carefully lifted out a large bottle of green leaves, flowers, and stems from the third shelf. Fred, you were quite right about the still, and now I have a good idea why she needed it." She pulled the cork out of the bottle, a strong, sweet scent filling the room.

"Smells like liquorice," Fred smiled.

"Correct. It is anise, one of the basic ingredients for both the candy and this." She picked up a small bottle of green liquid. She pulled out the cork and sniffed, her nose wrinkling. "Yes, just as I suspected. Absinthe. I had an idea we would find this somewhere here. Your beloved Green River drinks gave me an idea, and now I find I was correct. A French woman in an art community. It was the Green River the other evening that gave me the idea. The color is quite similar, is it not? Well, this is certainly an interesting revelation. I believe, gentlemen, we are getting a much clearer picture of our poor old Miss LeBeau."

"You solved the murder?" Fred asked.

Beatrix gave him a rare chuckle. "Not at all. But we have an understanding of the woman. The evidence is here. The still, the chemicals in this wardrobe, I could smell fennel when we first went into the kitchen, and of course, the wormwood out in the garden. All of the basic ingredients of this deadly drink."

"What about the poisons?" Horace asked.

"Amateurs sometimes used the poisons, especially arsenic, to enhance the potency of the hallucinogenic effect, what they called 'The Green Fairy'. It explains much," Beatrix said, wearing a slight smile of triumph. "She drank absinthe! Perhaps you remember the painting by Toulouse-Lautrec of Suzanne Valadon drinking it in a tavern. A number of Impressionists painted similar scenes."

Neither man was familiar with it and Beatrix continued her impromptu lecture. "The added ingredients, especially the wormwood and the other poisons, add to the mystique, as well as the thrill of trying to cheat death. Hallucinogenic, but potentially deadly."

"That solves everything except the three knives stuck in her back, and I'll bet dollars to donuts she didn't do that herself," Fred reminded her.

"Yes, well that is a challenge. However, we now know why the blood work and toxicology report presented such high poison levels. I was not surprised from the look of her fingernails. The striations were clear evidence; this just confirms the source."

Fred was about to remind her again about the knives, but Horace waved him off. Once again it was "Beatrix being Beatrix" as she single-mindedly focused on the pathology report.

"Before we close up that cabinet, I want to see if we can find another missing piece," Horace said. Without touching anything, he carefully examined the shelves and the wood of the cabinet. "Nothing here," he said. He pulled over a chair and was about to stand on it when Fred stopped him.

"Let me have a look-see, Boss. I'm a bit taller. "Up here on top of the wardrobe, huh?"

"Thunderation! You're shorter than I am by two inches," Horace reported.

"Might be, but I'm a lot quicker!" Fred said as he stepped up on the chair and looked at the top of the cabinet. "And lookee-here!" he said, "Feels like some old books. You want me to hand them down to you?"

"Yes," Horace and Beatrix replied in unison, and Horace added "That's the general idea."

Fred paused to look at the first one. "Looks like someone's notebook or something. Anyways, I can't make heads nor tails of it. It's not in English, that's for sure."

Horace took the book and slowly read his way through the first lines. "French. Looks like a diary. What do you think, Doctor?" he asked, handing the first book over to Beatrix.

"Well, if it is French, then I am out. German was my second language," she answered.

"You mean?" Horace asked.

"Yes!" she spat out. "There are some areas where my education is deficient. And that conversation is now complete!" Her face flushed even as the atmosphere in the room noticeably chilled. Horace and Fred knew better than to say anything else. Fred lifted down two more books and handed them to Horace.

The tension lessened only when Beatrix forced a smile and said, "So, if there is nothing else to be found now, perhaps we should take our leave, and look at these at the hotel."

Fred drove them back to town, Horace and Beatrix sitting in the back seat, as far away from each other as possible, both staring out the window on their side. At the hotel they walked silently up the stairs into the lobby. Horace watched as she stalked up the stairs to her room. He decided it would be best to wait.

A few minutes later Theo was coming out of his room as Horace walked up the stairs. "You don't look so good," he said.

"Rough time of it," Horace answered. He paused and sighed, "I think Beatrix is a little flustered, and for once it isn't my fault. I swear, I didn't say or do a thing."

"All right. Hard as it is to believe, tell me,"

"Well, we found some of Miss LeBeau's notebooks," Horace began. He handed them to Theo. "These."

"And?"

"Well, they're in French, and Beatrix said she didn't read French, and it set her off."

"Nothing too unusual about that, well, for most people, anyway. And you're sure you didn't say anything?"

"Theo, I swear. I kept my mouth shut. Thunderation!"

"Then just let her get over it in her own time. Better get used to it if you two are going to be, well, close colleagues. You might want to keep that in mind. Something of a new experience for you, isn't it? Caring about someone else's feelings? French books you say?"

"I'm pretty sure of it. Two of them look like old diaries."

"What's the other one?"

"It's strange. Little splotches of paint on the left side and more writing."

"Give them to me for a while. Clarice reads French like a Parisian, so she'll make some sense of them."

"Maybe we'll get a break," Horace said wearily.

"We could use one about now."

"You're right about that."

Theo watched as his brother slumped off to his room, closing the door behind him. In a few short hours Horace seemed to have aged.

CHAPTER NINE

Horace was stretched out on his bed, exhausted by Beatrix's sudden change, but unable to sleep. Three quarters of an hour later there was a soft tap at his door. It was she.

"May I come in? I must apologize to you," she said quietly, her face ashen and drawn.

"Of course. Wouldn't you be more comfortable in the lobby, though?" he asked.

"Under normal circumstances I would insist on it, but this is private. I behaved badly, and I must apologize. I hope you will forgive me." Horace held open the door for her, and she walked over to the desk and sat on the chair, facing the other chair where he sat. For a long time she looked down and didn't speak.

"This afternoon brought back a sudden flood of unpleasant memories. I was almost seventeen when I graduated from college, and my aunt, well, she thought I had spent too much time with my studies and had none of the social graces. Before I knew it, I was sent off to a finishing school in Switzerland to be trained how not to be so awkward around people." She looked up and flashed a brief smile. "I don't think it worked, do you?"

Horace said nothing. The news explained how she had so suddenly disappeared out of his life many decades earlier.

"It was the worst six months of my life. I did not fit in. That is the best way to couch it: I did not fit in. My clothing, my hair, I could not learn to dance, and I did not speak or read French. One of the nuns even took me aside to suggest I should forget about the outside world and become a Bride of Jesus, as she called it." She paused. "In other words, a nun."

"That's rough." Horace said quietly.

"I ran away half way through the year, to Berlin first, then back to the United States and shocked everyone when I was accepted into medical school. When I realized I had no bedside manner to care for patients, I specialized in pathology. I think you understand when I tell you that a laboratory is far more comfortable for me. Perhaps that is why you became a surgeon; your patients don't constantly prattle once you have put them under.

"It all came back this afternoon when you handed me the diaries, and I apologize for my behavior."

The two sat in silence for an awkward minute, neither knowing quite what to say. Finally, Horace said, "I understand all of that far more than you realize. For me, it's funerals of people I knew growing up and memories of the war, you know. All those young men wounded and dying. Long forgotten memories come flooding back. It's never comfortable, at least not for me. Now, my prescription is that you go back to your room, put on your war paint, and meet me downstairs for dinner. We march forward!"

Beatrix looked frightened. "I don't think tonight …"

"Now! A few months ago I went up in your flying machine and I was scared to death. I would gladly have paid that young taxi driver fifty dollars to drive me back to Saugatuck rather than go up in the air again, but I got in your plane. Dinner."

She smiled and got up to leave. "Thank you," she said quietly.

"And get a move on, woman. You know I don't like being kept in a waiting room!" he chuckled.

She turned around and smiled. "Did you know you are aptly named? I have been meaning to tell you for quite a while. Horace translates from the word 'timekeeper.' Perhaps that is why you hate waiting. You are a time keeper."

"And here I thought I was named after the Egyptian god who protected the kings," he bantered back.

"The spelling is quite different," she said firmly, not appreciating his pun. "I assure you, you are not a deity, even if your patients might believe that. In half an hour, then. I am not one of your patients. And, Horace, thank you. Again."

Outside of Theo and Clarice, Fred, Horace, and Beatrix, the dining room was empty. "Must be a slow night," Theo said.

When Beatrix was seated, Clarice turned to her. "These books are terribly dusty and musty. I'm surprised you didn't have an even worse reaction. My eyes have been watering all afternoon." She was rewarded with a thin smile from Beatrix

Theo looked over to Horace and winked. The crisis was over. Once again Clarice had worked her magic smoothing over ruffled feathers and hurt feelings.

"I have only had a chance to quickly look at them, but they are very interesting," she continued. "Two of them are diaries from when Miss LeBeau was quite young. The other one is quite different …"

She was interrupted by a waitress who brought water and single sheet typewritten menus. They spent a few minutes looking them over before the waitress returned. Horace, the last to order, was about to speak, when Beatrix said, "I believe I am correct when I say that Doctor Horace will be asking for whitefish." The table erupted with laughed, and a flustered Horace said, "Well, she's right. Whitefish, please."

"You were saying …" Beatrix said to Clarice.

"Two are diaries, and it is going to take a while for me to make my way through them. In what looks like the later one, her handwriting leaves much to be desired. And the third one is different. For one thing, the handwriting is very different. I don't believe it is hers. Also it appears to be a painter's notebook, a recipe book for mixing colors," Clarice said.

"If it is a color notebook, it should have the three primary colors at the beginning, red, yellow, and blue. After that the secondary colors. Red and blue make purple; blue and yellow make green, and so on," Beatrix said. "And then tertiary after that, and so on. Each one more complicated."

"Exactly. So, we confirmed that it is a painter's recipe book. Good. We have that established. So, the next question is who wrote it and how did Miss LeBeau come to own it?"

"With that woman, almost anything strange seems possible," Theo said.

"As I said, I went through it rather quickly, but there was a swatch of paint that caught my attention. I have never seen anything like it. A pale green. You know, in some ways it reminded me of those Green River drinks that Horace likes," Clarice said.

Horace and Fred looked rattled, Beatrix even more so. "Could you read what it was called?" Beatrix asked, drawing in her breath.

"Yes. Something called 'Paris Green Variation One.' There are two more after that."

Beatrix was silent, her eyes intently focused on Clarice, scaring her just a bit, the way she seemed to look through her. Beatrix shivered, and silently got up from the table and left the dining room.

"What in the world?" Clarice asked, bewildered. "The poor woman turned white like she had seen a ghost. Her own ghost. Does Paris Green mean anything to any of you?"

No one had an answer, but Horace had a strange inkling

"Should I go after her?" Clarice asked. "I wonder if she is alright."

"She will be just fine. I've seen that look before. She's onto something," Horace told her. "Nothing you said. She's thinking."

"Again," Theo muttered under his breath, weary of his brother always making excuses for her behavior.

A few minutes later Beatrix returned, carrying a large copy of "Chemical Formulary." Theo was about to ask, "A little light reading?" but thought better of it. She sat back down, pushing her table service to one side as she quickly worked her way through it. Suddenly realizing that the others were watching, she stopped, looked up, and said quietly, "The game's afoot." She returned to her research.

Horace burst into a smile. "See, I told you she's on to something."

It was only when the plates were brought from the kitchen that she dog-eared a page in the book and put it aside. As soon as the plates were removed, she lifted up the book and continued.

The others finished their meals, waited a few more minutes, and gradually excused themselves. Beatrix kept reading, oblivious to everything else.

"Stretch your legs, Fred?" Horace asked.

"If that means walking down for a fudge sundae and you're springing for it, I'm your man."

"Any idea what that was about?" Clarice asked her husband once they were in their room later that evening.

"Not in the least. I just know that if it had been one of our children you never would have allowed reading at the table like that."

"It was certainly peculiar. And what did she mean when she told Horace something about the game being afoot?"

"Oh, now at least that made sense. It's the two of them playing at Sherlock Holmes. She's as obsessed with the stories as he is, and they're constantly quoting something to each other."

"I see. Well, they are certainly very much alike," Clarice sighed.

"Just don't encourage them," Theo cautioned her.

"Why, whatever do you mean, dear?" Clarice teased. "I think it is rather charming, almost playful, and you know that is rare for Horace."

"You know very well what I mean. So, don't!"

Horace and Fred wandered back into the hotel a little less than an hour later. Beatrix had moved from the dining room to the lobby, still reading. "Don't interrupt her," Horace cautioned.

"Wouldn't dream of it. I gotta tell you, Doc, I'd like to get me a copy of that there book. Book that big has got to be a cure for insomnia," Fred answered.

CHAPTER TEN

"Fred, later on this morning I'd like you to run up to Holland and see some of those fellows you know at that tavern. See if you can find out if they know anything about a supply of absinthe around here. Supplies, seller, anyone who drinks that stuff, anything or anyone. It should be easy enough since it's French and they're all vets. They would have heard about it during the war, and I'll bet probably some of them would have drunk it."

"Yes, Sir!" Fred saluted. "Right away!" He was did an about-face to leave the hotel lobby when Horace called him back.

"Fred, I think it will work best if you wait until that place opens in a couple of hours, don't you?"

"Say, now, that's a good idea." He sat down again.

"I couldn't help but hear what you were saying, since I was listening," Beatrix interjected, "but before you go to Holland, Fred, I would like to go out to the LeBeau place and do a complete inventory of all the chemicals in the wardrobe. Perhaps you could drop us there?" Beatrix said.

"You on to something, Doc?" he asked.

"I am not certain," she said, looking into the distance. "I believe so."

Fred dropped them off in front of the house on the river, turned the car around on the narrow road, then went on up to Holland. For a moment or two Horace and Beatrix looked at the house. "Thunderation! We're a pair of green amateurs!" Horace snarled in disgust. "I just realized there's a second floor." He pointed up to two small windows with brownish lace curtains.

Beatrix nodded in agreement. "We are worse than Inspector Lestrade! But I did not see a stairway or a hatch and ladder," she said as she stared at the windows.

"That's because we never went out back because of the poison ..."

"Hemlock," Beatrix finished his sentence. "That is why we missed it! Oh, we were being careless."

"Well, let's see what's outside the kitchen door, then. My guess is we'll find an outside stairway to get up there."

The two of them walked through the house and gingerly opened the back door. "So far, so good. No booby traps and nothing that looks poisonous out here climbing up the stairs," Horace said with relief. "Shall we go up?"

They paused at the foot of the stairs, Horace waiting for Beatrix to go first. "Do you mind?" she asked. When Horace didn't respond, she nodded down to her blue skirt. Horace smiled and carefully went up the unpainted wooden steps to a small landing, certain any of them would collapse under his weight, and opened the door. He was about to go in when Beatrix pushed passed him, staring in shocked silence at the room. She swallowed several times before quietly whispering, "This woman needed an alienist more than I thought."

"They're called psychologists today," Horace corrected her.

"In her day they were alienists, and she definitely needed to spend some time as a patient. Just look at this room."

"A bit garish and badly decorated, if you ask me, but what are you seeing?"

"A complete, perfect recreation of Vincent van Gogh's rooms in Arles. He lived there for a while and decorated it for Gauguin before they parted company. It is a total recreation. How odd. How very, very odd. The same wooden bed, the same color on the walls, even reproductions of the paintings he did and hung on the walls. And look, over there, painting supplies, canvas, everything." Beatrix was almost panting in excitement. For a moment she did not realize she was leaning against Horace for support. "It's as if we stepped through Mr. Well's time machine into another time and place."

"Alright, but I'm falling behind — again," Horace said. "Why are those two fellows so important to her? And why here? It doesn't make sense."

"For some reason van Gogh idolized Gauguin and created this very room …"

"This room? Here?"

"No, in southern France. He painted two, perhaps three different paintings of the room. I've seen one of them, and this is exactly what it looked like," she told him. "It is like walking into the painting."

"More like joining Alice tumbling down a rabbit hole, or ending up in Oz with Dorothy," Horace barely whispered. "But why?"

"I have no idea. She must have thought she had to keep their memory alive or something. I have absolutely no idea what she was thinking. All I know is that this is not the behavior of a rational human being. In a museum, perhaps, but in a private home … ? How very odd. And yet, somehow electrifying."

"Maybe Clarice will find something in those notebooks," Horace said, walking over to the table. He was about to pick up a container of paint when Beatrix told him not to do it. "Do not touch that! Do not touch anything. Not now, anyway. We must see if we can make any sense of this, first. Do you have your notebook with you?"

"Yes," he reached in his suit pocket and pulled it out. Beatrix turned to a blank page and made a quick sketch, then handed it back to him.

"Did you know that before the war all telephone operators and secretaries were men?" Beatrix asked.

"Yes. Many were, at least." Horace wondered what made her think of that question.

"Good, then you would also know what a secretary is and does? I believe you have just volunteered to be my secretary. Write down the names I give you, please."

For the next ten minutes Beatrix looked at every item on the desk, quietly and distinctly telling him what he was to write. When she finished she asked him to read the list back to her, checking each item off the contents of the table. Satisfied that her work at the desk was complete, she moved on to the paintings on the wall.

"And this is interesting," she barely whispered, looking at the back of one of the paintings. "The linen is old, from the looks of it. And these large headed brads appear to have been used before. Yet the stretchers are quite new."

"Perhaps she was a thrifty painter," Horace suggested.

She looked up at Horace. "It does not appear that she is a painter. Notice that there are no little spills or paint she has wiped up. Not on the table, the floor, anywhere. And no turpentine or rags to clean her brushes. It is not her studio. It is a recreation of van Gogh's studio!"

"Odd is hardly the word for it. This is a sign of a very disturbed woman," Horace said quietly. "It almost makes the witchcraft idea make sense."

She smiled. "Good. Now, back downstairs and we can inventory the wardrobe. This is becoming very exciting!"

Horace wasn't sharing her enthusiasm.

For a second time the two of them carefully looked at every bottle and jar, with Horace taking down notes. When Beatrix came to the last one, she turned around with a puzzled look on her face. "This simply does not make any rational sense. Outside of everything here being poisonous, and some of the bottles being very dangerous, there does not seem to be a pattern nor logic here."

"We're missing something. We're *still* missing something. Every time we turn around, this is getting more and more complicated. It should be simple. Murder is simple, and it is always rational, if only to the murderer," Horace said softly. "I don't know about you, but I'm ready to get out of this death trap, sit down, and think it through." He looked at his watch. "You realize we've already been hear several hours?"

"We can take the chain ferry back. It is only a couple of hundred yards down to the landing. Of course, you did not bring your walking stick did you? Do not bother answering. I know you did not, you mule-headed country doc!" Beatrix teased.

"Start walking," Horace teased back, a smile on his face. "And on the subject of walking sticks, I saw how your back was a bit stiff yesterday. Well, Fred brought along a second walking stick, and you're welcome to it,"

"I'd rather be flying," she said, almost wistfully, ignoring his gentle offer. "You know, if I had my plane here we could fly over this place and see it from a different perspective. It might help."

They were waiting for the chain ferry to come across the river when Fred pulled up. "Thought I'd find you somewhere over here," he smiled. Horace and Beatrix got in the car.

"Any luck up in Holland?" Horace asked.

"Well, yes and no. I struck out when it came to that liquor you wanted to know about. No one has ever heard of it. Sorry, boss," Fred said.

"In a way, I am not surprised. It is French and that is a Dutch community. I doubt it would have been part of their culture," Beatrix added.

"Well, it was a long shot from the start," Horace said. "Anything else?"

"I think so. I ran into a fellow who wants to meet up with us in two hours. He said we were to pull up at that airport where you landed last summer, Doctor Howell."

"That sounds mysterious," she replied, her eyebrows shooting up in excitement.

Clarice was sitting in a rocking chair on the front porch of the hotel, so focused on her books that she didn't notice Fred pull up to let his passengers out.

"Well, any luck making sense of her diary?" Horace asked.

Clarice put down the diary and said, "I don't know. I think I've forgotten some of my French, but some of it seems to be coming back. I may be missing a few words, but I've got the gist of it. I don't know what to make of it. If it's a young girl's fantasy, she has an active imagination, for sure. And if it's the truth, well, I don't know what to say. It's bizarre."

"Salacious?" Beatrix asked.

"No, it isn't that way. Not at all. It is, well, it is a very strange diary. Some parts are confusing, and some seem very morbid. And did you look at the third book, the recipe book?"

"No," both Beatrix and Horace replied.

"I think you should. Perhaps you can make sense of it. The first half is filled with formulas for mixing colors like we talked about last night, but the last pages are something else. And as I said, the handwriting is different, too." She handed the third book to Beatrix. "It matches the diaries!"

Beatrix sat down to look at it, slowly turning through the first pages, then skipping to the back. She looked at Horace and Clarice. "Oh, this is strange. It is definitely interesting but strange," she said anxiously. Her voice weakened, "Very, very strange."

"Why?" Horace asked.

"It's a jumble of formulas and recipes …"

"French pastries?" Horace asked.

"You wish!" Beatrix answered. "No. Chemical formulas and recipes. Some of them appear to be for mixing paint. Others are entirely different. I despise speculation, but all things considered, we need to be open to the possibility that these were the formulas that van Gogh might have used to mix his paints."

"What do you mean?" Horace asked.

"We have established that the two diaries and the last pages of this book are by the same hand — the same person. The first part of this book is by a different writer. All things considered, perhaps van Gogh. It is a distinct possibility after seeing the bedroom."

"Why van Gogh? He was a famous artist, so why wouldn't he have purchased his paints?" Clarice asked.

"I am quite sure he wanted to buy them," Beatrix told the group, "but remember, during his life, he only sold one painting. As an artist, he was a complete failure until after he died. He's famous now, but when he was alive, no one knew of him. I don't think he could afford them, and so he probably mixed his own. Some of the formulas might even date back to the Middle Ages."

"And our little chambermaid wrote all this down?" Clarice asked, still puzzled.

Beatrix answered, "No, I suspect this might have been van Gogh's recipe book. Most artists have one, so that is logical. If this can be authenticated as his, it is extremely valuable. Museums and collectors would pay a fortune for it. But then there are several blank pages, almost like a division, and the rest of it is in her handwriting, and that is the very strange part. There are some more formulas for mixing paint, and more sketches and drawings, but the rest of it is in French. I am afraid, Clarice, you will have to guide us. We can do that later.

"Horace, please go away so I can study these formulas. If I can find a pattern to them, we may have the key to her life, and perhaps why she was murdered."

"What are you looking for?" he asked.

"I am not certain" she said slowly. "I hope to find a different pattern between van Gogh's formulas and the ones in the back. If I can, they may be from another painter. If they are from a different source, then we will know much more."

"Fine. But know what?" he asked, puzzled.

"I do not know. Please, go away and let me concentrate."

"In a minute. There's another possibility. What if our Miss LeBeau found van Gogh's recipe book, realized there were blank pages, and used it to hide some information in the back?" Horace asked.

"What sort of information?" Clarice asked.

"I don't know. Something secret, maybe in code, she wanted to hide from others," he answered. "It could be anything."

"Horace — go away!" Beatrix snipped at him.

"All right. Fred and I'll be back in about an hour and a half."

"And take your walking stick with you. You've been on your feet most of the day," she said without looking up from her book.

Horace chafed at being instructed as if he were a child, but dutifully sent Fred up to his room to get his walking stick.

"Can't see why you put up with her," Fred said as the two of them started walking down Butler Street. "She can be rude as anything."

"She's not rude; just very focused. Anyway, I don't mind. Sometimes, well, it's worth it. She has an interesting brain. Let's go to the Parrish's and have a Green River. My treat. And you can tell me about this mysterious man we're going to meet."

Even after being plied with a Green River, Fred refused to tell Doctor Horace anything about the man they were to meet in a little less than an hour. "All I'm saying is that we're to be out to the airfield to meet him."

It did not leave his employer in a good mood. "I've had my fill of mysterious information for right now. It started off with Phoebe and her dead crows, then a dead woman, and now van Gogh, Gauguin, and these confounded diaries she kept. Thunderation! Why in the world can't this fellow you met just come to the hotel like a regular Joe? Fred, this fellow wouldn't be some friend of yours out of Chicago, would he?

"I don't think so. He talks like those Texicans. You'll see soon enough."

Horace paid for their drinks, left a quarter tip and said, "Well, let's get back to the hotel so we can go meet this mysterious man. And you think he's going to have some answers for us?"

"No, Sir. Now, I never said that. Maybe he is and maybe he isn't."

"Wild goose chase, if you want my opinion," Horace snarled, ending with an explosive "Thunderation!"

"Come on, Theo, you too. And Clarice, you've had your nose in those books long enough for a while. Come on with us," Horace commanded. "Everyone pile in." He held the door for Beatrix to get into the passenger seat.

"Fred, are you going to tell us what's going on?" Theo asked.

"Nope. Not yet. Just you wait and see. You folks are worse than children on Christmas Eve waiting for Santy to come down the chimney. You gotta wait a while longer," he chuckled.

They had just stepped onto the grass at the edge of the runway when they could hear the sound of a plane far in the distance. Horace noticed how Beatrix wheeled around and cupped her hands over her eyebrows to scan the sky, focusing on the direction of the sound.

"Oh, my! There it is!" she exclaimed when she finally spotted it, pointing her left hand in the right direction to a little dot far in the distance. It was still out of sight for the rest of them, and finally came into view.

All of them watched as the plane began to descend. It came down low, circled the grass field, then pulled up and circled once more to land. "It is beautiful!" Beatrix said. She was so entranced she didn't hear Fred whisper to Horace, "Wait 'til she sees it up close and who's flying it."

The plane taxied closer, then pivoted 180 degrees to face away from them. "It's a Lockheed! It's their newest model!" Beatrix said as the pilot shut off the motor. "I believe it is their new Vega!"

The canopy opened and the pilot stood up, waving to them. "Hi-ya, Fred, old buddy. Good to see you again."

"Friend of yours?" Horace asked.

Fred tried to be casual. "Ah, just somebody I happen to know. Now keep your eyes on Beatrix."

Even standing behind her they could see her right hand swing up to clap over her mouth. She wheeled around. "Do you know who that is? Do you? That is Wiley Post! One-eyed Wiley. He gave me my first aeroplane ride!" She was jumping up and down with unbridled excitement. Theo was speechless at first, watching her. "Didn't know she had that in her," he mumbled. "She's always so reserved."

Calm, confident, and with a smile on his face, he sauntered over to them, his right hand extended. "Wiley Post, and if I'm not mistaken, you're Doctor Beatrix Howell. You drove me out to Wold Chamberlain a few years back when I was in the Twin Cities. Don't know if you remember, but I'm kinda surprised to see you down here."

"Remember? Remember you?" Beatrix barely croaked out. "How could I forget? You gave me my first aeroplane ride."

"Ma'am, I didn't think that was the first time you went up. Usually folks are pretty scared their first time. They stiffen right up and hold on for dear life, some turn white as a sheet, and a few get airsick, but you took to it like an ace. First time, huh? You sure had me fooled, then. Say, I got a new plane since the last time I saw you. Remember the old one? Stearman C-3 by Boeing. This here's a Lockheed — their new Vega. Want to take a look at the cockpit?"

"Yes!" she clapped with joy. "May I?"

"Course you can. That's why I gave you the invite. My buddy Fred here tells me you're a flying fool. When I saw him today we got to talking, and that's when I found out you were here. He said you'd be pleased if I dropped in. Guess I must have been a bad influence on you. So, whatcha got?"

"I have a Stearman C-3, with a modified engine and larger fuel tanks."

"Well, that may be older than this one, but you can't beat them for reliability. Leastwise, that's what General Billy Mitchell told me. Come on, I'll take you up if you folks got time to cool your heels a few minutes," Post told them.

"No, not at all," Horace said. Theo and Clarice looked at him as if he was crazy.

"I do not want to impose. I can walk back if you want to be on your way. I will not mind, trust me!" Beatrix offered.

"Wouldn't dream of it," Horace chuckled. "You two go have a good time."

"Look, I'd take all of you up with me, but dang, this field has a short runway. Might not make it." He nodded in the direction of some trees near the far end of the runway.

"That's quite all right," Horace said, relieved that his feet would stay on the ground.

Horace, Theo, Clarice and Fred watched as the two of them walked over to the plane. "A little jealous, big brother? You're taking a real risk she might fly off into the sunset with him." Theo teased.

"Happy for her, and even happier I'm not going up in that thing."

Post started the engine and taxied to the far end of the runway, and the others could hear the engine straining against the brakes as he revved it to full speed. The moment he released the brakes, the plane hurtled down the grass, and whipped up into the sky. "Bet she's having the time of her life," Clarice said, still waving at her long after the plane was gone.

While the two pilots were flying above the Kalamazoo River on their way out to the lake, Horace turned to Fed and asked, "And just how long have you and Old One-eyed Wiley been such good friends? I don't recall you mentioning him before. Ever."

Fred reached for Horace's left hand and looked at the wristwatch. "Oh, I'd say we've been pals for maybe three, three and a half hours by now. I said I'd top off his tank if he'd come down here to take Beatrix up, and he was right happy to oblige. I figured it might be good for her. Just the same as I'd be obliged if you'd give me a couple of ten-spots to pay for the gas." He smiled broadly. "And that would be good for me."

"Well worth it!" Horace laughed. "And well done. That's awfully thoughtful of you."

They watched as the plane came back again, still over the water, when suddenly the engine seemed to stop, and the plane began to glide toward earth. "They're going to ditch in the water!" Horace shouted. A long ten seconds later, the engine came to life again, and they gained altitude, climbed and circled, and then once again settled down on the grass. This time Post left the engine running as Beatrix clamored out and stepped back on the ground.

She shocked them by blowing him a kiss, and then waving with both hands as he taxied to the far end of the field, turned, and took off. He wiggled-waggled the wings as a final goodbye, sending Horace's straw boater skimming into the weeds. Fred dashed to collect it for him.

Beatrix was ecstatic, breathing hard, her face flushed with excitement, and her right hand over her heart. Theo reached for a small silver flask in his coat pocket to give to her.

"I am fine. No. No thank you. I am quite all right," she said as she began to calm down. "That was so exciting! What a wonderful machine! He was right: it does make mine look like an old fashioned toy. You should see all the instruments and gauges. It boggles the mind. Fred, thank you for running into your friend again and asking him to come down."

Beatrix was so excited, for a moment Fred was afraid she might kiss him on the cheek.

It was only when they were in the car on the short drive back to the hotel, waiting for the swing bridge to lock into place, that Clarice said, "We thought for a moment we were going to lose you. What happened? The engine stopped or something. Horace was as white as a sheet."

"White sheet, indeed!" Theo thought. His wife was playing fast and easy with the truth.

"No, not at all," Beatrix gulped. "That was intentional. And, it is important. When we were flying down the river we went right over the LeBeau house. Horace, you remember, I said I wanted to see it from the air and get a different perspective. And the other day, Fred, you said you thought you found a place along the bank where someone had been pulling in with a canoe? You were right!

"The canoe was there, and I thought I saw someone in the grass, prone, trying to hide from us and watch the house. Whoever it was did not move. So, when we came back, Mr. Post turned off the engine. He said that a man could stay still if a plane was going overhead, but if the engine suddenly quit, they could not resist seeing if something was wrong. He told me about helping a lawman named

Tilghman, a William Tilghman, yes, that was his name, find an escaped prisoner in Oklahoma. And, he was right! It worked! Just after Mr. Post turned off the engine, he turned over to see us!"

"So, someone is watching the house!" Horace said.

"Exactly. And we flushed him, just like Mr. Post and Marshal Tilghman did."

"And that means we're on to something," Horace said quietly. "We finally got our break."

"Yes, exactly. And I believe this is where you are supposed to say, 'It is a good thing I brought along my gun,'" she told him.

"Oh," Horace said, not quite comprehending her.

"Well, did you? Did you bring along a pistol? A 'piece'? Is that not what they call it in Chicago?"

"Oh, I understand. Yes, it's in the grip up in my room. And, before you ask, yes it's loaded, and extra bullets."

"Good. Bring it along the next time. And your walking stick."

"I have mine, too," Theo said grimly.

"Got mine!" Fred added.

"Theo, I don't like this. Not one little bit," Clarice said.

After Fred dropped them off in front of the Butler Hotel, Clarice turned to the others. "I hate to change the subject just now, but I think I've got more news for you."

A MURDER OF CROWS

CHAPTER ELEVEN

"So tell us what you learned, Clarice, before we interrupted you by going out to the airfield," Horace said after he had moved a chair in the lobby closer to where she was sitting. Theo, Fred, and Beatrix moved closer, as well,.

"Well, apparently our Miss LeBeau was employed as a chambermaid …"

"We already know that part, Clarice," Horace reminded her.

"Well, here's the interesting news: A few months after she began working Vincent van Gogh arrived …"

"I just knew it all along! Thank you for confirming it!" Beatrix suddenly interrupted, then settled back, still broadly smiling, her eyes closed in joy. "My apologies. Please, go on …"

Clarice continued. "Apparently, the two of them got along quite well and befriended each other. She obviously found him exotic and unusual. The older man had travelled, was a painter, and probably was quite different from the men her own age. She wrote about how van Gogh painted the portraits of the two daughters in lieu of his rent, what he ate, that he was a bit odd, and so on. Apparently, she was one of his very few friends. In two separate places she mentions that she went into the village tavern with him, and that he introduced her to absinthe. Apparently, the last time several men from the village taunted him, he got very drunk, and she had to help him home.

"But here's the real kicker. She wrote that on July 27th, 1890, she was cleaning an upstairs chamber and looked out the window across the fields. A couple of boys were hunting or target shooting with their guns, when one of them fired in van Gogh's direction, probably just to scare him because they knew he was, well, mentally tetched in the head. Everyone in town thought that of him. They didn't scare him. They hit him, probably by accident. The bullet struck him in the abdomen. It must have been a small calibre because he managed to get back to the hotel and made it up to his room."

"Stop! Stop right there! That cannot be right!" Beatrix said sharply. "Van Gogh himself said that he wanted to commit suicide, and that he shot himself with his own gun! That is what he told the police. This is a different story completely. That cannot be right. She must be making this up to protect his reputation!"

Clarice nodded in acknowledgement, then continued. "She wrote that the police were called and van Gogh said that he tried to commit suicide." She paused, letting the news sink in, and saw Beatrix relax slightly.

"If her story is true, then in other words, he was covering for the boys from the village. He must have had the presence of mind to know that the wound was fatal. It also means he knew that if he lived and he told the truth, they'd go to prison; if he died, they'd go to the guillotine," Beatrix said quietly.

"And everyone believed the story because there weren't any witnesses. Well, except for Miss LeBeau, and she kept quiet. That changes the entire story," Theo said. He let out a long low whistle. The rest of them remained silent, thinking over what Clarice had just told them.

"The poor woman. I can just imagine van Gogh begging her, making her promise not to say anything. And yet, there he was dying and his reputation being destroyed," Clarice said gently. "How very troubling for her."

"You haven't told this to anyone else, have you?" Horace barely whispered.

"No. No one. We are the only living people who know about what really happened that July afternoon. Well, the only ones who know what Miss LeBeau wrote in her diary as a witness."

All of them sat in silence, still trying to absorb the story.

"So, does that mean the dying van Gogh either gave his paint recipe book to our Miss LeBeau or she stole it before or right after he died?" Horace asked. "One way or another, she got her hands on it."

"Well, she doesn't tell that part. Just that he died in absolute agony, and that when they cleaned out his room the owner gave her two paintings to compensate her for cleaning the mess …" Clarice said. "It's just a guess, but perhaps the hotel owner let her have the book, or for all we know maybe tossed it out and she got hold of it later."

"Or any number of ways," Theo said.

"Slow down, Clarice, Horace advised. "When you go through the diaries the next time, see if there is some mention about how she got effects. It would seem to me that she would mention it if he gave them to her, seeing as how she is so besotted with him.

For the moment Beatrix was not interested in speculating about how Miss LeBeau acquired the book. It was the mention of the paintings that held her attention. Her eyes flashed in surprise. "The ones we saw in the bedroom! They are two of his wheat field paintings. Real ones!" Beatrix exclaimed. "They … are … genuine!" She could barely get the words out.

"What bedroom?" Theo asked.

"Later," Horace said. "Go on Clarice. Then what?"

"Not much that isn't well known. His brother Theo, not you, dear, came to make arrangements for the burial, and then a few months later Theo died, probably from drinking himself to death. They're buried next to each other in the village."

"So, it's possible that Theo might have given our Miss LeBeau the diaries," Theo said.

"Yes," Beatrix said, "But not relevant at the moment."

Fred let out a slow whistle, "I got an idea that might wrap this whole thing up. So, someone done Miss LeBeau in to get their hands on the diary. That explains everything. They knocked her off to keep her quiet, but never found the book with the true story! Well, that's something."

"No, Fred! Wait a moment!" Beatrix snapped. " I believe you have it wrong. Clarice, earlier, you said that in the recipe book you found his formula, instructions, for making his unique shade of green. Do you realize what that means? She has, well, that is, had, the formula to make van Gogh green! The only person to know the formula and how to do it."

"That's important? How?" Horace asked. "None of this is making much sense. I can see covering up an accidental shooting. Keeping a couple of pretty pictures makes sense. But the idea that she knows how to mix green paint, well, it can't be that important."

"Horace," Beatrix said, "it is far more important than you realize. It is the most important part of all! No one wanted his paintings when he was alive, but after he died, people snapped them up. They are priceless now. Imagine, owning two of his wheat field paintings. That alone is a treasure. But, what has always captured the imagination of artists and collectors is the tone of his green. Artists have tried, but they have never replicated it. Supposedly, there is only a small amount of his original green anywhere in the world, and even that is probably a myth …" her voice trailed off.

"Except …" Theo said softly.

Beatrix turned to him. "Yes. Anyone who does use the same green claims that they have the original paint from van Gogh himself, although it is highly doubtful. That makes it exceedingly rare, if, as I said, it even exists anywhere today!" Beatrix explained. "I have examined many paintings. Some were close, some were very close, and once in a while, almost perfect, but never truly perfect."

"Only our little Miss LeBeau has, or rather had, the formula," Horace added, his voice low. "And all the ingredients …"

"And two priceless paintings," Clarice said in shock. She clapped her right hand over her mouth.

"When we were in that bedroom and inventoried everything, there was no green! It was the only missing secondary color! I did not think of it at the time. There was no green!" Beatrix exclaimed. "Everything on that desk was an exact recreation of the bedroom paintings, except for the green!"

At first, only Beatrix could fully comprehend the implications. Even Horace was clueless and had a vague idea that it had to be something significant and important, something worth murdering an old lady.

"His unique green is missing. Either she used it, lost it, or it was stolen the night she was murdered. I doubt it was the latter, which can only mean that the van Gogh green no longer exists, and she was attempting to duplicate it from his book. I would have to do a long and intensive investigation to prove it, and I could only do it in my own laboratory," Beatrix said.

"Why?" Horace asked.

"I fly solo, remember? If I borrowed another laboratory, or if I had an assistant, then sooner or later the secret of my work would be out …"

"And that puts you in danger," Theo answered. "I see what you mean."

"More than that, far more! Discovering two new paintings by van Gogh is one thing. I have done that with paintings someone thought was a fraud, and I have determined some paintings an owner thought were real were fakes. More often it is the other way around. This is far more than that. If Miss LeBeau did have the formula to make the paint, then it would set off an earthquake among artists, dealers, historians, insurance companies, and no telling where it would end. It might ruin collectors who paid very high prices for van Gogh's paintings because of his green. Galleries and auction houses would lose their credibility. Curators would be disgraced. Lawsuits would go on for years."

"And it would consume the rest of your life," Horace said gently. "I understand. At least I think I do."

She sat silently for a long minute before quietly adding, "And, to be honest, it would be the end of my privacy," Beatrix said, her voice almost desperate. "No one must know what we have discovered. At least for right now. Maybe not forever, but at least right now. We must keep this to ourselves! Please, all of you, if you value my friendship, you must not tell anyone. Please!" There was a look of desperation in her eyes as she turned from one person to the next.

"Agreed," Theo said. The others added their pledge.

"As if that isn't enough, there is more than that to consider," Clarice said quietly and slowly. "Those two young boys. If they are still alive, they would be old men by now, but they might still be tried for murder. The murder, even an accidental one, of a famous artist.

Even if they are dead, they might have married and have families who are still alive — widows, children and grandchildren. After all these years, decades, really, the notoriety and shame that they killed van Gogh would destroy them."

Her words silenced all of them as they instinctively shifted their chairs closer together. "I was a lot happier investigating three dead crows," Horace said, forcing a chuckle.

"A little late for that now, Sherlock," Beatrix said flatly, unable to force even a wintry smile. "We are in a tight fix. We need time to think and analyze all of this before taking any action."

One by one they seemed to settle back and slump in their chairs, thinking in silence.

"Alright. The first thing is we agree to say nothing about any of this to anyone other than among ourselves. That includes Harriet and Phoebe. No one," Horace said firmly. "Absolute silence."

"To keep the secret?" Clarice asked.

"More than that. To stay alive. Beatrix told you what she saw up in the plane. Someone is watching the house. We don't know who it is or what they want, but someone knows something or thinks they know something. Now it's starting to get dangerous. I think we are all in grave danger."

Beatrix breathed a sigh of relief because the others were beginning to understand. "Yes, we are all in danger," she said quietly, looking down at her lap. "I am sorry. I somehow feel I got you into this. Please forgive me."

"So, we're all in a bit of danger right now," Horace repeated. "That's why I want Harriet and Phoebe left completely in the dark. Is that clear? They're far safer that way. The way I see it, we don't know who's watching the house, or anything else, or who they might be working for."

"Shouldn't we tell Chief Garrison?" Theo asked, moving his chair closer to the others.

"Not yet. We should, I know. Sooner or later we'll have to, but not yet," Horace said. "I don't think he would understand any of this, and he certainly wouldn't keep quiet about it. Right now, he can't be trusted with this news."

"I agree. Not until we know what we are doing, and more importantly, what we are going to do," Beatrix added. "Absolute silence, even if we are on our own."

"Our next challenge is what to do with those three books. As far as we know, no one knows we have them. And if we are lucky, even the Meldens next door don't know they exist. Even if they suspect their might be diaries, they don't know that we have them. We have to keep it that way. Fred, would you go over to the front desk and ask if they have a safe?"

They watched as Fred stood up, then walked across the lobby, talked to the bellman for less than a minute, and returned. "Yeah, they got one."

"Good. Now, Harriet and Clarice, by any chance did either of you bring a small jewelry box along with you, large enough to hold the books? We'll need to borrow it."

"I did, but I didn't bring anything valuable. I didn't think I would need it," Clarice said.

"Yes, I did, too," Beatrix said. "Mine is just paste, not gemstones."

"Good. That's very good. We will need them both. Clarice and Beatrix, I'd like you to take out anything you might want to wear for the next day or so. When you have done that, Clarice, bring the box to my room and go back to your room. After that, Beatrix, come to my room with your box and I'll hand Clarice's off to you to put it in the safe here at the hotel. Fred, I want you stay here and keep an eye on the place. Watch who comes in and who goes out. After Beatrix puts the box in the safe, I want you to keep watch for another ten minutes. Keep an eye open for anyone you haven't seen in here before. Understood? And keep an eye on the desk clerk to see if he telephones anyone. Just come back over here and sit for a while."

"Yes, Sir!" Fred said with a smile of delight.

"All right, but, but what about the other empty box?" Clarice asked. Horace ignored her.

"Theo, you and Clarice and I are going over to the Fruitgrower's Bank and put Beatrix's box in a lock box in the vault. All three of us will have to sign the card so that any of us can retrieve it. I'm afraid it means you'll have to do your reading in one of their private rooms at the bank, Clarice."

"What about my notes? The ones I took this afternoon?" she asked.

"Those, too. We have to lock them up. No traces. It's too dangerous to keep them in the hotel and even more dangerous to have them on you if we get waylaid. We've got to lock it all up, at least until we know more," Horace smiled. "Oh, and my notebook, as well."

"Oh my, so I'll be out-flanking the enemy! How very exciting!" Beatrix said, surprisingly cheerful.

"Not quite, Doctor Howell. You and I are a diversion," Fred explained. "It's a triple-switch razzle-dazzle."

"Well, it is still rather exciting. I have never been a diversion before!" Beatrix said, quite pleased with her assignment. Theo tightened his lips and turned his head before he said anything about Beatrix being too much of a diversion to his brother.

"All right. Everyone knows what they're doing. Any questions? Hearing none, then let's go to work. Everyone knows what to do?

Good. Harriet and Clarice, switch jewelry boxes. Theo, slip the books beneath your waistcoat. Fred, you stay here. Beatrix, ten minutes after you put the box into the hotel safe, take your time walking down to the Green Parrot to meet us for coffee.

"Green Parrot is going to be closed by now," Fred said.

"All the better. We'll meet out in front and go for a walk."

"In that case, you had better get your walking stick," Beatrix told him firmly. "And, your pistol."

"What do I do after ten minutes?" Fred asked.

"All right. They've got some Chicago papers at the desk. Ten minutes after we leave, pretend that you're bored just sitting around in the lobby, get up and buy one, then come back here and keep watch. If the clerk asks anything, say that you didn't feel like going for a walk. Pretend you're reading a newspaper, but keep watch for anyone who comes in, talks with the desk clerk and leaves, or goes up the stairs without a key in his hand."

"You want me to get my revolver ready?" Fred asked.

"No, no need for that this afternoon. Just keep watch, and don't give yourself away," Horace told him. "And everyone relax and look natural. Fred, you're on guard duty while you stay in the lobby until we get back. Better go down the hall now, just in case. There won't be an opportunity later. Fifth door on the left."

Half an hour later the four of them were standing in front of the cafe. The sign on the door said "closed". A bit louder than necessary, Horace suggested, "So, let's stretch our legs, shall we? Let's stroll down Water Street to that little park. By then Phoebe ought to be home from school. Maybe we can have another dinner together tonight."

"Not much to see at that park," Theo grumbled, still uncertain what his brother was doing, and thinking a lot of it was nothing more than stage-acting.

"We might be surprised. It's fifty yards or so up and across the river from Miss LeBeau's house. No telling what we might learn," Horace said.

"You took my notes on the supplies we found in the wardrobe. We forgot about putting them in the bank box. Thunderation!" Horace said softly to Beatrix.

"I didn't forget about them. Don't worry, they are safe and secure," Beatrix answered.

"Where?"

"I would prefer not to say, if you do not mind," she whispered, her face slightly blushing.

Clarice gave her a knowing smile.

Theo was right. Once they passed a couple of abandoned fish shacks, there wasn't much to see at the park." More like undeveloped land fit for snakes and mosquitoes," Theo sniffed, as he swatted one off his right cheek. "I can't possibly imagine anyone not wanting to live next to a fish house. Horace, you'd love it — close to your precious whitefish. Say, Clarice, how'd you like us to buy this lot and build a house right here?" he teased.

"No thank you. I got used to you smelling of ether, antiseptic and no telling what other hospital aromas all mixed with carbolic soap. I didn't mind it. Fish, I can live without. But, now if you want a little place all by yourself, you go right ahead."

They stood looking at the water. Theo noticed Horace nod his head toward the dock. Tied under it, partially out of sight, was a canoe. They said nothing. Horace pulled out his watch and looked at the time. "Well, let's see if Miss Phoebe is receiving."

CHAPTER TWELVE

They watched as Phoebe and a young man were slowly walking up the street, the lad obviously so smitten with her that he was willingly carrying her books. When Phoebe realized they were being watched, she was surprised and uncomfortable, obviously embarrassed and took back her books. She coughed and introduced her friend, "This is Henry. We're in class together and he lives in the next block."

Horace reached out his hand. "A pleasure to meet you, Henry."

"Are you Phoebe's grandfather, Doctor Balfour?" he gulped in discomfort.

"I am. And this is her great uncle, another Doctor Balfour and Mrs. Balfour, and this is Doctor Howell."

"You're here to solve the mystery of the dead crows! Everybody's heard about it! They all want to meet you, Sir. Have you solved the case yet?" he asked.

"I believe we have a theory," Beatrix suddenly said. "Do you want to explain, Doctor Balfour?" Her question startled him, catching him off-guard.

"No, no. You started. You go right ahead and finish. I'd like to hear you explain it — again," Horace said quickly, trying to make a quick recovery.

"Henry, do you ever eat apple seeds or cherry pits?" she asked cautiously.

"Well, sometimes by accident. I was trying to spit out a cherry pit once, but got the hiccups and swallowed it. Is that bad?"

"Yes and no. You really should try to be careful never to eat them, and never do it on purpose. The seeds contain a chemical that, when it mixes with all of the gastric juices, that is, all the liquid in your stomach and intestines, it becomes a poison called cyanide," she slowly explained.

"I thought that's how you got a burst appendix. That's what my buddy Stu said when he had to have an operation," Henry answered.

"Well, I am not sure he was right. But if you eat too many of those apple seeds or cherry pits you can poison yourself. Many people do not know that and eat them, and sometimes they become ill. But, crows do not know it. There are a lot of fruit trees here, and we think maybe the crows ate too many seeds, and that was what killed them. Does that make sense to you?" she asked.

"Yeah, I think so," he said quietly. "I ought to get home and get my chores done. Stu and I are going to haul out the clinkers at our house and then go over and do his." He hurried down the street without saying goodbye.

"You ever haul clinkers out of an old coal burner?" Fred asked Beatrix, but before she could answer Phoebe interrupted.

"Is that true, Doctor Howell, or were you teasing about apple seeds?" Phoebe demanded.

"It's very true," Horace answered for her. "So, no eating seeds, young lady? Is that clear? And make sure your friends know it, too."

"And that's what killed the crows? Eating seeds?"

"Well, we are not finished with our investigation yet, are we, doctors?" Beatrix asked. "Right now that seems to be the likely cause."

"Is that true, grandfather?" Phoebe asked again.

"Doctor Howell is a brilliant pathologist. She knows more about poisons than I do, so I'll take her word on it. Maybe she's got some good advice."

Phoebe thought it over for a few moments.

"That's something you can tell your class tomorrow," Clarice added. "It might be a good thing if you did."

"Say, Phoebs, we're just out for a stroll. How about telling your mother we stopped by and want you two to join us for dinner this evening? About six or so? Want to do it?" Horace asked.

She looked up at him. "If you promise not to say that Henry walked me home from school."

"Promise. We all do, don't we?" he asked, looking at the others, waiting for them to nod in agreement. "We're experts at keeping secrets! Tell you what, why don't you ask her to call the Butler and they'll tell us at the front desk whether you can join us or not." Horace saw Beatrix hiding a slight smile, realizing the double meaning of his comment about keeping secrets.

"Jake with me, then!" Phoebe smiled, spitting into the palm of her left hand and slamming her right fist into it.

"Jake with me, too!" Horace replied, repeating their ritual. He smiled when both Clarice and Beatrix gasped in dismay.

"That is not very sanitary," Beatrix announced.

"Nor very gentlemanly, either," Clarice added. "Beatrix, is that true about apple seeds?"

"Yes, it is very true I believe one would have to eat a considerable quantity before becoming nauseous, much less poisoned. However, I believe it solved her curiosity, if only for a short time."

They continued their stroll down the street, and when they were away from anyone else, Horace asked his brother, "You saw the canoe?"

"Yeah," Theo said.

"It could be the same one. I did not get a good look at it from the air," Beatrix said. "The angle and distance are different from the ground."

"Well, it's in a perfect location. If someone were watching from this side of the river, they'd see us from that old shack long before we got there. They'd have time to paddle over, land, and crawl up to watch us."

"Too bad there's only one road. There's no way to get past our sentry," Horace said.

"Well, Fred could drive us up that old fire trail to the water tanks, and then we could slip down through the woods," Theo suggested. "Fred might have to back down if there isn't room to turn around once we get up there. And probably plenty of chances to get hung up if the trail is rutted."

Clarice gave him a stern look. "I don't think so. Besides, he'd see the car long before we got there."

"Well, what say Fred drops us off, then drives up further toward the water works building, parks the car, and then crawls down the bank and hikes along the shore and sneaks up behind him?" Theo asked.

"Fred would love it, and you know he's going to say that's what he did when he were fighting the Hun. That's how he captured all their field marshals one afternoon," Horace said. "So, the answer is 'no'. That idea might work if it were dark. Our spy, well, if he is a spy, would see him coming down the shore long before he got there and he'd take off. Besides, did you see he left a fishing pole in the canoe?

He can always pretend to be fishing if we try flushing him out. It creates a good alibi, even if he is up to no good. Keep thinking," Horace told him. "Better yet, don't think about it, and for heaven's sake, don't give Fred any ideas!"

"So, Phoebe tells me you may have figured out what killed those crows she's been going on about. Apple seeds, really? That's on the level?" Harriet asked as she slid into her chair next to Clarice in the hotel dining room a little after six thirty. She arched an eyebrow, wondering if they were teasing the girl.

"You can thank Beatrix for that," Clarice said.

"And you're truly serious about apple seeds?" she asked.

"Definitely. You might want to say something to your students," Beatrix told her. "That might be all the more timely since it is the season for apples."

"I'll speak to the principal about it first and let him make the decision. So, you'll be going home soon, or is the death of Miss LeBeau your next mystery to solve?" There was a tinge of frost in her voice.

"Oh, we'll give it another whirl or two. There isn't much to go on, and it is far more than merely a death. It is definitely a murder," Horace said, trying to be cheerful.

"What I can't understand is why she became a victim. She never mixed in with the community or seem to have any friends. No one knew her or had a grudge that I know of. She was the wall flower of all wall flowers. And from what I've heard, her house was little more than a hovel, so it can't be worth much, so it couldn't be for her money because she didn't have any. If this were Salem, Massachusetts people might have thought she was a witch, but, well, that's all nonsense and hysteria out of the past."

Harriet didn't see the look of surprise on Clarice's face. She visibly recoiled and blanched. Beatrix and Horace noticed, and Horace abruptly changed the subject. "So, Phoebs, what are you studying in school? Start with history. That's always interesting."

"Oh, some ancient Greek fellow named Archimedes. He said that if he had a long enough big stick he could move the entire world. But that doesn't make sense, because where would he stand?"

"Archimedes, huh? Well, I don't think he really intended to move the earth. He was making a point about how to move things," her grandfather replied. Horace glanced over at his brother who was suddenly lost in thought. "You'll understand it much better when you study physics."

Beatrix abruptly changed the subject when she asked Horace if he was having whitefish for a second night in a row. He was, and she said she would do the same. Something seemed to be troubling her, and she shivered several times.

Right after dinner Harriet said it was time to go home so Phoebe could go to bed and get her rest for school the next day. They all walked out to front door, and watched them go down the steps, turn and wave, and walk down the street.

"I have got to get out of this corset," Beatrix whispered to Clarice.

"Too much dinner?" she teased. "Or was it the apple pie and ice cream?"

"No. I put the notes I took out at the house in it for safe keeping. The paper is poking into my … into me. And please don't tell that to Theo."

"I promise. Your secret is safe with me. Look, next time wrap the notes in some of your hankies if you're going to do that," Clarice suggested. She watched as Beatrix hurried toward her room.

"Say, come and join us in my room," Horace called after her. "Fred's got a surprise for us."

Beatrix waved and said she would.

"Just in time," Horace said. "Fred, you want to do the honours? Just a small one all around." They watched as Fred filled their glasses. "It's Haig, blended from Scotland. The real McCoy."

"Cheers!" they said quietly to one another as they lifted their glasses. No one dared to ask where he had scavenged it.

Beatrix interrupted them. "Harriet said something that caught your attention, Clarice. Something about witches in Salem. I saw your reaction."

"Well, I started telling you about it earlier. In Miss LeBeau's books are some drawings. Sketches, really. Very strange drawings of stars, daggers, and what looked like very bizarre ceremonies of some sort in what almost looks like a pagan temple."

"Are you saying maybe our Miss LeBeau was a witch, or someone thought she was a witch, and that's why she was killed?" Horace asked. "I hadn't thought of that angle."

"No, probably not. However, they are certainly dark and foreboding, and about two thirds of the way through there were some names I didn't recognize," Clarice continued. "Péladan was one that kept turning up. I didn't get to read much more of it, but he seems very dark and frightening. When Harriet mentioned witches, it caught my attention."

Beatrix turned white, her eyes widening, and she shuddered hard and started trembling. "I don't want any part of that," she barely whispered. She was silent with her head down until the color came back to her face. "I know the name Péladan," she said slowly and quietly. She put her glass, still untouched, on the table and quickly left the room without a word.

Clarice got up and followed her down to her room. "I will be alright," Beatrix said to her when they got to her door. "I need to be alone and think."

"What do you know about this Péladan? Tell me …" Clarice said.

"He was an evil genius."

"And? I'm sure there is more."

"And dangerous. Please, I need to concentrate. Alone." She quickly went into her room, closed and locked the door behind her.

CHAPTER THIRTEEN

Clarice returned to Horace's room in less than three minutes, the rest of them anxiously awaiting her. "She'll be alright, but this business needs to come to an end," she said harshly. "Solve it or quit. And soon. I mean it — for her sake."

"Why? What rattled her?" Horace asked. He was about to add that he didn't believe he had said anything to upset her, but thought better of it and remained silent.

"I did when I mentioned the word 'Péladan'. And don't ask questions because I don't understand it, much less who he or she was. I've never heard of him, and all Beatrix would say is that he was evil. Evil as in satanic. She knows a lot more than she's letting on, at least for right now. It definitely rattled her. So, you three be gentle tomorrow, is that clear? And solve this or cash in your chips."

"Yes, yes, of course," Horace said quietly. "Anyone have an idea who or what this Péladan is?"

"No, not really, but he must have some sort of a connection with van Gogh and the paintings. Beatrix obviously is aware of him, so it has to do something with art. It's too bad the notebooks are locked in the bank, or I could read more and perhaps find out," Clarice told him.

"I know. But, from what you just said, I'm all the more convinced that having them around here isn't safe. For all we know, he might be the man with the canoe who's been spying on us."

The four of them sat in silence, thinking. Fred removed the revolver from his pocket and checked to make sure it was loaded. Theo shook his head at him to tell him to put the gun away.

Horace began slowly, almost as if he was thinking out loud. "Alright. Tomorrow we'll go back to the house again. Let's hope Beatrix is up to going. Phoebe gave me an idea that might work. Archimedes didn't just work with levers. He used mirrors, as well. Look, when we're ready to go, Clarice, I'd like to have Fred drop you off at Harriet's house. We'll wait until they've gone to school before we start. And, Clarice, make sure you have a mirror with you …"

"There's a compact in my handbag with a mirror," she interrupted.

"Good. That's all we'll need. Now, you can see the road and Miss LeBeau's house on the other side of the river from their porch. I know because I checked this afternoon and there's a direct line of sight. And the good news, you can't see Harriet's porch from that fishing shack.

"Now, it'll take a few minutes for us to get over to the other side. If the fellow with the canoe is watching us, he'll come across the river the moment he sees us down at the swing bridge. So Fred, see if you can time it so he can get into position before we get there. If he does, then Clarice, wait until we get to the house and that's when you signal us with your mirror."

"What good is that going to do?" Theo asked. "He's still got the advantage on us."

"Maybe, only this time we'll know for sure he is there watching us, and he won't know that we know," Horace answered. "Like I said, Phoebe mentioned Archimedes and his lever. Well, the old boy also used an array of mirrors to burn enemy ships. We don't need to burn that fellow's canoe, just signal us that he's behind us."

"And then what?" his brother asked. "What good is a little mirror going to do?"

"We nudge the odds a bit more in our favour if he's watching us and we know it. And if he comes across the river, then we'll know that, too, so we can be ready for him. We'll have to wait and see what his next move is. After that we'll do what we've always done — make it up as we go along."

"Or, we could flush him out and get the jump on him," Fred suggested.

"We'll see when we get there. And fellows, we'd better be sure we're armed and on guard," Horace said firmly.

"What do I do once I've signalled you?" Clarice asked. Before anyone could answer she suggested, "There's a chair on the porch. I can stay there and keep watch. If your man makes his move I can tell Chief Garrison to get over there right away."

"Good idea. Harriet has a telephone now, and she keeps a spare key over the doorframe. I suggest you find it as soon as you get there. Check to make sure you can unlock the door and get in the house. The telephone's on the wall in the kitchen."

"How exciting! Breaking and entering! I've never done that before. It's almost as good as being a diversion, don't you agree?"

Theo reached over to take his wife's hand. "I think you make a great diversion." She giggled and kissed him on the cheek.

"You up for this?" Horace asked Beatrix the next morning over breakfast.

"Yes. I must apologize for my reaction last evening. Péladan is a name that terrifies me. Some of his followers, disciples, minions, really, were even worse. When Clarice mentioned a drawing with three daggers …"

"And now three daggers in the victim's back …" he said softly. The two of them stared at their coffee and Horace added, "You don't have to come along, you know."

"No. No, I must. We are getting close to resolving this. And, I need to face this devil straight on. Just tell me you have your revolver with you and that you will be on guard."

"I do," Horace assured her, putting his hand on his right coat pocket. "And I will. Promise."

"If it is a matter of safety, then I'd rather be with you, Fred, and Theo than be on my own," she tried to smile.

"All right then, let's go. But listen, if this gets to be too rough, Fred will get you out of there and bring you back here straight away."

"Thank you, Horace," she said quietly.

He realized she had still not told him why Péladan was so dangerous, nor anything about his gang. The Péladan Gang was unfamiliar to him. The Chicago Outfit and Purple Gang, those he knew. There was a small gang of Norwegian safe crackers, the Cream Can Bandits, working out of the Twin Cities, hitting small town banks. The Péladan Gang was a new one. Horace knew this was not the time to pump Beatrix for more information. She'd clam up if she felt uncomfortable.

A little after 8:30, they put their plan into motion. Fred dropped Clarice off at Harriet and Phoebe's home, then drove back to the Butler Hotel to collect the others. Seven minutes later they were across the river and driving up Park Street, slowly making their way toward Miss LeBeau's house. "Take your time, Fred. We want to give him plenty of time," Theo advised. "If he's even watching," he muttered in disgust.

When they got to her house, Horace climbed out of the car slowly and stiffly, then stood to stretch as he scanned the houses across the river. "In-coming," he whispered after seeing a series of flashes from Clarice's mirror. He pretended to stretch his right arm and shoulder, signalling back to Clarice that he had her message.

"Now what?" Fred asked. "If you want, I'm pretty sure I could slip in behind him."

"No, you stick with us. Look, when we get inside, just be ready. All of us," Horace told him. He nodded at Beatrix to proceed.

With a louder than usual voice Beatrix said, "This time, let's make sure we get all of the rest of the paint. Check everywhere. We've got to take it out now and then get out of here."

As they started up the front steps Beatrix suddenly grasped Horace's arm and squeezed hard. "I have been meaning to tell you about all the bottles of poison. At first I could not make sense of them. I just realized she has all the ingredients for making 'Paris Green'. Arsenic, copper acetate, the bottle of cadmium yellow, and the rest of it. It is all deadly poison."

"Paris Green is that same stuff that van Gogh used, I take it," Horace whispered.

"No. Almost. She's added cadmium blue pigment. She must have figured out it is the other ingredient to get the right tone. Finding the right mixture of the cadmiums would have been the only challenge left. It was the hard part. I remember looking at the book. All the other paints had a ratio; his green did not. My guess is she mixed it in her kitchen, then tried matching it against the paintings upstairs in her bedroom."

"And if she got it right, she would have made a fortune," Horace said, adding a low whistle. "So, while we're at it, let's see if we can find her stash."

Beatrix froze as they stood at the doorway, and without thinking, Horace set down his walking stick just outside to steady her. "Let's go," she whispered. "I just realized there is method to her madness. The front parlour is a filthy pigsty to keep anyone from going further into the house. They would not want to go into the kitchen, assuming it had to be worse than this."

"And the poison hemlock was to keep them from prowling around in back and going up the stairs! Horace added. "That makes sense."

"It does. It really does," Beatrix said, sucking in her breath. "Oh my! She was clever."

"Keep your eyes peeled for a hidey-hole," Horace told Theo and Fred. "It could be anywhere in here. Inch by inch, boys, inch by inch."

"You realize that with all the arsenic in her system we're not dealing with a rational mind," Theo said.

"I've been thinking that since the start, even before we learned about the arsenic," his brother answered. "At least not consistently rational."

"And she'd be far worse near the end," Theo added.

Fred busied himself lifting pieces of filthy clothing and rags off a chair, checking for clues and finding nothing. "Struck out here," he said, pushing the chair out of the way so he could get to the next pile. The floorboard creaked. "Loose board like that needs to be nailed down" he fussed. "A man could stub his toe on that if it popped up."

"Thunderation! No it doesn't," Horace said. "Pull it up. You might have found what we're looking for!"

Theo and Beatrix joined Horace as Fred slowly pulled on the nail, lifting a board squeaking in protest as he pried at it with his jack knife. Between the joists were three quart bottles of green liquid. "Don't touch it; use this," Beatrix cautioned, handing him a rag from the pile. "Use this and be careful not to spill anything or drop it. It's all poisonous."

"You want these jars first, or this little leather pouch?" Fred asked. "Feels kind of heavy."

"Pouch," Horace said. "Watch yourself."

"Don't worry about that. Them Huns booby-trapped everything they could lay their hands on." He gingerly felt beneath the bag, hoping not to find a firing pin to a small mine. "Clear," he breathed in relief, wiping a shirt sleeve across his forehead. "You got to hand it to the engineers. They did this all the time during the war. Nerves of steel, those boys."

The three of them peered into the opening while Fred, on his hands and knees, gingerly lifted out the leather bag. He loosened the draw strings. "Well, what d'ya know! Filled up with gold and silver coins!"

"Lift out the jars, please. Carefully," Beatrix said, completely ignoring the cache of coins.

Using the old rag, Fred lifted out the first quart and set it on the floor.

"Oh!" she exclaimed. "It is beautiful, even if it is deadly."

"That's what we've been looking for! Thunderation, Fred! You did it. We have it!" Horace said clapping his hands.

"Not for long!" a voice said from the doorway. "I'll take that. Move aside and get your hands up and keep them that way!

The four of them obeyed, mortified that they had been so interested in the jars they had forgotten to keep watch on the door.

"That there is a sawed off shotgun," Fred said. "We'd better do what he says."

"A sawed off shotgun is very illegal!" Beatrix objected. "It is against the law for you to have that! You could be arrested just for owning that, young man!"

"This isn't the time to discuss the finer points of the law," Horace whispered softly, trying to calm her.

"I think it is!" she retorted. "That type of gun contravenes the law!" She turned to the gunman and snapped, "You should be ashamed of yourself! Your mother would be disappointed in you! Very disappointed. I know I am. Shame on you!"

"Lady, you're crazy. You're a crazy lady! Now shut up!"

Beatrix was quiet for a moment then snapped at Horace. "Do you realize this is the second time this year we have been ambushed and had someone pointing a gun at us? I am sure your mother would be disappointed in you, as well. Do you realize how careless you have been? Do you?"

"Well, yes," Horace said quietly. "We'll discuss it later." He thought, "if there is a later."

Beatrix was relentless. "You promised me there would not be any gun play this time! You promised, Horace Balfour! You gave me your word!" Despite the instructions from the gunman not to move, she ran her right index finger against her nose, winking her left eye.

Horace understood what she was doing and was willing to play along. "Now, if you remember correctly, I only promised I would try not to let it happen. I didn't say it wouldn't happen; just that I'd try. Well, it didn't work out the way you wanted it. Woman, you can't have everything your way all the time!"

"Why do so many people want to shoot you, Horace?" she asked. "Just tell me! Why?"

"Later," he repeated, once again hoping there would be a 'later'.

"Doctor Howell, if you knew my brother better then you'd know there are a lot of people who'd be quite happy to take a shot at him. You just stick around with him long enough, and you'll be thinking the same way," Theo told her.

"Shut it! All of you. You're all acting like loonies. I got a gun, remember. Now all of you, keep quiet. I'm running things here. Shut it up or I'll shut you up for good!"

Theo turned toward the young man with the gun. "Just who are you, anyway?"

"Let's just say I'm business partner of Miss LeBeau," he answered, stepping further into the house. "We had a real sweet heart of a deal. She gives me a shopping list, and I buy what's on it and bring it here. She mixes up that green paint for me and I buy it for a pretty penny from her and then I got some clients who pay me the big money to get their hands on it. Artists, painters, quality people like that."

The man looked at the three jars and the pouch on the floor. "Looks like I don't have to pay this time and get a refund on my money," he laughed.

"You realize that Miss LeBeau is dead. There won't be any more paint," Theo said.

"As if I care. And I don't. You don't get it, do you old timer? There's a fortune in that pouch and it's money I gave her. And, those jars are worth ten times as much. I play my cards right and parcel it out nice and slow, and I'll make even more. After that, I'm on easy street and fixed the rest of my life."

"You'll be fixed up in a noose if you shoot us," Theo said firmly. "Did you kill the old lady, too?"

"Nah, I knew she was holding out on me for more money, but I didn't kill her. She was my milk cow so I just played along and waited. I knew my time would come. Looks like it has. Besides, she was crazy as they come, a real alky, drinking that green liquor all the time. I knew it wouldn't go on forever, but now that I've got the money back and the rest of the paint, I figure it don't matter.

"All right, lady, I want you to slide that money bag over here to me. Nice and easy. Remember, I got your friends covered. Do it!"

Beatrix did as he commanded.

"Now, take some of those rags and wrap up those jars, and then tie them up in another piece so I can carry them out of here. I'm not touching that stuff! Get a move on. I don't want to be here all day. Places to go and people to see, like they say." He leered at her.

Beatrix carefully and methodically wrapped the first two jars, the gunman alternating his attention between her and the three men.

Horace saw the flicker of a shadow outside on the porch. Someone else was there.

"Can I help you?" a voice said from behind the gunman.

The gunman turned a quarter of the way around, carelessly lifting the shotgun up towards the ceiling as he looked over his shoulder. The man behind him rammed the heavy head of Horace's silver walking stick up between his legs, causing him to flinch and scream in agony, and pull the trigger. The shotgun roared, deafening them, the buckshot shattered the ceiling and sent plaster and a cloud of dust to the floor. Instantly the man brought the walking stick down across the side of gunman's head, knocking him out cold. He tumbled onto the floor with a heavy thud.

"Very happy to see you, Mr. Melden," Horace said as calmly as possible, his fluttering hands betraying him. "How'd you know …?"

"Well, I saw him come in behind you. I've been keeping an eye on him, figuring he might be up to no good. Guess I was right. He's been hanging around the past week or so. I caught on to him staying in that old fish house 'cross the river. Afore that, I'd see him a couple a times around town. I never did think he was up to any good. Guess this just proved it. First time I seen him with a scatter gun, though. Got to admit that."

"No idea who he is?" Theo asked.

"Nah. None. Like I said, he'd turn up around here once in a while to see Miss LeBeau," the neighbor answered. "I figure he might be a relative or something like that."

"And she never said anything about him?" Horace asked. "He said he was her business partner."

"Nah, not her. She mostly kept to herself the last few years. She didn't like us nosing around, so we kept her distance. Well, the missus would look in on her once in a while, like I told you, but that's it. So, what happens to this fellow? You think he murdered her? I guess we ought to call the police." He was staring at the hole in the ceiling.

"Thank you for saving our lives," Beatrix said quietly, her eyes down. She was shaking. Theo offered her his flask, and she took it from him She gasped after a small sip, handing it off to Horace. Fred and Theo finished it off.

Mr. Melden nodded to her, acknowledging her gratitude.

It took Fred only a few seconds to regain his presence of mind, and bent over to pick up the gun. "Oh, that's much heavier than I expected, what with a short barrel." He opened the breach to extract the two shells, then set it aside. The others were still too shaken to talk.

"Shall we wake our visitor up?" Fred asked. "Maybe a little cold water would help."

When no one answered he went out to the kitchen to get a saucepan of water, pushing the leather pouch across the floor until it tumbled into the hidey-hole. When he returned he unceremoniously threw the water over the unconscious gunman. The man sputtered and moaned in pain. Fred pulled out his own pistol. Theo and Horace did the same.

"I think the odds have changed, so maybe you'd like to start singing like a canary," Horace told him. "Before the police chief gets here. He'll have a lot of questions for you, including why you murdered Miss LeBeau. I suggest you start talking."

The man looked up at him, then the others, snorted in derision, and refused to speak.

"Mrs. Balfour was watching across the river. She signalled us, and by now she's called the police chief," Theo explained. "So, you best know he's on his way. Anything you want to tell us before he gets here? Might go easier on you if you fessed up."

Fred added, "And I'll bet you plenty that just about everyone in town heard your shotgun go off, so they'll be calling the police chief, too. Say, what you want to bet that we're going to have an audience here in no time?"

"I didn't have nothing to do with that, with killing the old lady, I'm telling you!" He shouted, then settled down. "We had a business deal, straight up. She made that green stuff, I bought it. That's all there is to it."

"I see," Horace said. "Theo, you ever know of any paint salesman who hid out in an empty fish shack and went around with a sawed off shot gun?"

"Nope. They might carry a brush or one of those little paint paddles, but never known one to carry a shotgun. They usually don't travel around in a canoe, either," Theo answered. "Looks like the chief is going to have a lot of questions for him. A lot."

"Say, they might carry one of those little palette knives, though," Fred added, chuckling at his own joke. "In case they get into some sort of dust-up." Horace just shot him a hot look of disdain. " Yeah, you're right, Boss, the chief will give him the old third degree under the bright lights, alright, and with a rubber hose," Fred added. "They always talk — sooner or later. Course, they might not look so good after they get roughed up with a piece of hose."

The gunman on the floor sneered at Fred.

"Tough guy, huh?" Fred asked.

The man merely glared back in defiance, and remained silent.

It took the chief and a deputy just under ten minutes to get out to the LeBeau house, delayed at the swing bridge while a boat came down river. "So, we got our murderer!" he said, clapping his hands. "Soon as he signs a confession we'll have this case closed up nice and neat. You folks better follow me down to the station house so I can get your statements. And stay right behind me. I don't want you talking to nobody about nothing until then."

He snapped a set of handcuffs on his prisoner and gave him a hard push out the door.

CHAPTER FOURTEEN

The four of them and Mr. Melden had watched as Chief Garrison handcuffed the gunman and put him in the back seat of his police car, instructing one of his officers to keep an eye on him and not let him make a run for it. "See you down to the station," the chief reminded them as he slid behind the steering wheel.

The chief turned to Mr. Melden and said, "I'll be back out here after I get our murderer booked and all settled into his cell. I want a statement from you, so stick close to home."

"I'll do that. Better go back before my woman thinks she's a widow or something," he said, giving the chief a wave.

"Looks like the chief forgot to take the evidence," Theo said, shaking his head in disbelief, looking down at the leather pouch and the three jars of paint. "Pure carelessness. Well, we can't leave them here unattended." Fred carried out the paint, putting the jars in the trunk of the car, and then shoring them up with the spare tire so they wouldn't tip over. He closed the top, then leaned against it.

"Getting a bit old for this sort of tom-foolery," he said to no one in particular while he waited for the others. He glanced toward the Melden's house, just in time to see a slight movement in the lace curtain in the front parlor. He was being watched.

"These go too," Beatrix said, panting from running up and down the back steps. In her hands were the two paintings from the bedroom. "Thank you, Fred."

"Lady, you sure are a glad hand when it comes to pinching someone else's paintings. You remember this summer out to Ox-Bow?" he asked.

"Yes, and now I am doing it again. They are too valuable to leave unlocked. Please be very careful with them. They are priceless." She watched as he gingerly laid them in the trunk, then covered them with a blanket. Together they gently closed the trunk and leaned against it. "Fred, look over at the window," she whispered.

"Yup, I know. I saw it earlier. Someone's curious about what's going on," he whispered back. "Probably nothing more than curiosity."

Beatrix said nothing, but she wasn't certain Fred was right.

All four of them were drained from their experience. Theo sat in the front seat, silently watching the passing scenery; Horace and Beatrix sat close to their doors on the back seat, both of them staring out the windows in opposite directions, lost in their own thoughts. Fred understood no one felt like talking, and he drove in silence. Finally, he said, "I can't get over the chief, leaving all the evidence right there on the floor, and keeping his officer outside so he could claim all the glory." No one answered him.

When they got to the police station, Clarice was waiting for them, almost instantly wrapping her arms around Theo's neck in relief. "I could hear shooting from across the river," she told him. "You have no idea …"

"I know," Theo said quietly to her. "Everything is over now. It's okay. We're safe and sound. Now, look, the first thing we have to do is go to the cop shop and give our statements. Soon as we're done, we'll be right back."

"Are you sure it's all over? I heard a gunshot," Clarice repeated.

"It was not shooting," Beatrix said flatly. "There was just one shot. Well, perhaps two shots since he fired both barrels of his shotgun." Clarice ignored her.

Theo gave her another hug and kiss. "Looks like you're stuck with me a while longer." He gave her a third hug and told her he'd meet her back at the hotel.

"While I talk to the shooter, you four start writing. And, no talking, neither. I want your statement in your own words, you hear?" the chief instructed. "When you get done, make sure they're signed and hand them in to my secretary. After that, you're free to be on your way."

"Remind you a little of school?" Horace quipped. "Sounds like our old mathematics teacher when we were growing up. You remember his name?" he asked Theo and Beatrix. Theo shook his head. Beatrix said quietly, "Walloo. Mr. Herbert Walloo. He did not like me, and the feeling was very mutual."

"Yeah, well let's not go traipsing down memory lane, at least not now. Let's get this done and over with. I'm tired," Theo answered. He started writing, then looked up. "Mr. Walloo didn't like anyone."

It took Horace the better part of an hour to finish writing his statement. Beatrix finished about the same time. "Catch up with you back to the hotel," he told Fred and Theo when he stood up to leave. As they were going out the door, Horace turned, "We're the good children who got their homework done first!" Theo stuck out his tongue at him.

"Theo's not the only one tired," Horace told Beatrix as they walked out the door of the station. "I'm knackered. You?"

"Yes, surprisingly so. Absolutely drained. I felt quite alive at Miss LeBeau's house, but now all I want is to retire for the rest of the day," she told him. "It was quite exciting, was it not?"

"Hope you don't mind a quick stop at the drugstore. Say, that was quite the little show you put on, distracting the fellow that way," Horace said. Beatrix didn't answer. "It was a show, wasn't it? I mean … ?" Once again she remained silent, smiling to herself. She found it amusing to perplex him from time to time.

"Please, don't even suggest one of those awful Green River drinks. Not now," she sighed. "I don't think I want to see that color for a very long time, and they taste awful!"

"No, not that. Pipe tobacco and matches this time. How about a cigar or two for you?" he asked.

"I am very sure that must be against the law."

"What's against the law?"

"A woman smoking a cigar in public."

"Oh, come on. It might be against the law somewhere, but if you read the ordinances here in Saugatuck, about two thirds of the way down, you'll see there is an exception after a woman has helped capture a felon," he teased.

"In that case, I would like three." She flashed a quick smile, leaving Horace confused as to whether she was serious or not.

When they were out on the street in front of the pharmacy Beatrix turned serious again. "Horace, you know we were very nearly killed — again. That is the second time this year. Did you see the damage the shotgun did to the ceiling? That could have been us, you realize."

"That has come to mind," he told her.

"It is not amusing, Horace Balfour. There are times when I do not find it safe being with you. I am not certain I want to accompany you on any more of your adventures," she said in carefully measured words.

"But you'd miss the excitement. It's a bit like going up in your aeroplane, if you think about it."

Beatrix said nothing in response, thinking it over and realizing that he was right. She would miss the excitement.

Wearily, the two of them started up the front steps when Beatrix put her arm on Horace's sleeve to stop him. "Something is not right. I do not know what it is, but it is something important. I think we've missed something."

He looked at her and nodded. "I know. I've been thinking about it, too. We're missing a piece of the puzzle. That man with the shotgun wasn't the killer. I'm sure of it. I just can't get a handle on what it is. I can't see my way through it."

"What are you going to do? We cannot let an innocent man go to prison," she said almost desperately.

"I don't know; but, no, we won't let that happen."

"Or beat up with a rubber hose, or worse … ?"

"I think Fred was just trying to scare him a bit. Don't worry," he told her. "There's an ordinance against that."

"That might not be sufficient," she reminded him.

They had been on the porch for a quarter of an hour when Fred, Theo, and Clarice returned from the police station. Even from a half block away Theo could tell his brother was lost in thought and decided not to interrupt him. Then he changed his mind, walked over to where Horace and Beatrix were sitting and slipped him his silver flask. "Might help," he whispered. Horace just nodded, taking a sip and passing it to Beatrix.

"Thought we drained it out to the house," Horace told his brother.

"We did, but Fred …" Theo answered.

"Of course he did," Horace smiled as he watched her take a small sip. She screwed up her face at the taste of it, and handed the flask back to Horace.

"We were just talking. We think we're missing something. The whole thing feels odd; just plain wrong," Horace told Theo.

"I agree with Horace. And it is something right in front of us." Beatrix looked around, and seeing no one on the porch or street, took the flask for a second quick sip. "It is so obvious it's a three-pipe mystery trying to see it." She handed the flask back to Theo.

"Or a three cigar mystery," Horace quipped. He turned to his brother and added, "We'll be inside in a few minutes."

After the others left, Horace turned to Beatrix. "One thing that puzzles me is that the chief thinks it was a simple case of murder. You know, the three knives in her back. And yet there is no apparent reason why she would be murdered. Yet everything we know — the toxicology report, that cabinet, the diaries, in particular — make it very clear that she was trying to create van Gogh's green. He's off on the wrong track. I wish I could figure it out."

She flicked the ash off her cigar and took another long drag, slowly blowing out the smoke. "I am not certain I agree with you. There is the matter of Péladan, and the drawings of his devotees known as the "Decadents". She may have been claiming to make the paint in order to cover her desire for revenge. The opposite is possible, too. Maybe she was murdered by another of his followers. And remember, Horace, poison is often a woman's choice of weapons."

"Beatrix, you know a lot more about this Péladan than you've told us, and I haven't pushed because it troubles you. I think the time has come …"

She sucked in her breath and barely whispered, "Yes, I should tell you." She looked down, perhaps trying to form her sentences, then very quietly and slowly said, "Péladan was a genius. He came from a wealthy French family and probably did not have to earn a living. His brother certainly did not worry about money. The brother studied the occult and alchemy. When our Péladan moved to Paris to work as an art critic and writer, he was obviously influenced by his brother and before long he also began dabbling in the occult. From what I understand, it was not long after that he consulted with Tarot card readers and others of their ilk. Either he became quite adept at giving readings, or it was sheer showmanship. Perhaps a combination of both. I would not be surprised, but I suspect absinthe played a role in clouding his brain, because he proclaimed himself the Grand Magician. The man was charismatic and he ruined many lives …"

Her voice trailed off, and she became almost catatonic, staring straight ahead, her cigar growing cold. "Many good people, perhaps even great artists, succumbed to his charms. From what I have heard from others or read about him, it was almost as if he took delight in their pain."

Over an hour passed with the two of them staring off into the distance, silently thinking. They were interrupted by a very animated Fred. "Boss! Sorry to barge in on you like this, but I got big news and a lot of it."

"What?"

Fred pulled up a chair to join them. "It's like this, Doc. With all the excitement this morning and then having to write my report when we got back here, I forgot to ask at the desk if we had any company. You know, someone wanting to see us or something like that. I'm sorry about that, real sorry, on account of the fact that we done did have someone looking in for us, but I don't think that any harm has come out of it, even if I'm telling you just now. The fellow at the front desk said that someone came in and asked for your room number. He said you weren't in, and they said that you wanted them to get something out of your room and bring it to you right away, so the bell hop handed 'em the key.

"Well, I borrowed your key again and just went up to check, and sure enough, someone's been in there, and that's for sure. Messed up, and right smack dab in the middle of the floor is that box we were playing pass the present with the other night. Empty! If there was something in there, then they done did steal it."

Beatrix turned toward Fred, her eyes wide open in shock. "I thought it was in the bank vault!"

"Just a minute. I'll explain," Horace told her, then returned to Fred, "And did the clerk tell you the name of this man? A description? Anything?" Horace asked.

"Man? Who said anything about it being a man? It sure weren't me. The clerk said it was a woman. He didn't get a name, but she said she was your secretary! Weren't no man. It was a woman! A woman of the female persuasion!"

Horace listened carefully, and then a smile flashed across his face. "Fred, get the car! Irene, on your feet! The game's a-foot. We have to get out to the LeBeau house straight away!"

"You know who did it?" she asked. Horace didn't answer.

CHAPTER FIFTEEN

"Horace, I demand to know what is going on," Beatrix said forcefully, turning around in the front seat of the car to talk to him. "Especially if someone is going to shoot at us again."

"It's the missing piece. We have it, and I doubt there will be any gunplay now."

"You still have your pistol, I trust?" she asked anxiously.

"Yup."

"Please do not let them get the drop on you again. Once today is enough." Her voice was urgent and serious.

"Now look, before we get there, if there is anything more you ought to tell about us this Péladan and his gang, start talking!" Horace practically barked at her.

"Only that you are partially wrong. Péladan does not have a gang. He had followers in France forty years ago. And, he died just months before the war," Beatrix said firmly.

"And you are quite sure he is dead?"

Beatrix stared out the window. "From what I know of Péladan, it is never certain. But yes, I believe he is dead." Her words did not reassure Horace.

Both Fred and Horace instinctively felt their jacket pocket, reassuring themselves that they were armed.

When they pulled up in front of Miss LeBeau's house, instead of going inside, Horace led Beatrix next door and knocked. "Fred, stay out here, please. We may need you," Horace instructed. "And keep watch for any more unexpected visitors."

"Yes, Sir. I'll keep a close eye on our rear to make sure they don't get the jump on us! You can count on me," Fred answered with a salute.

Mr. Melden answered the door, surprised to see them again so soon. "I was wondering if we might come in. I have a question or two for Mrs. Melden," Horace abruptly explained.

He invited them into the front parlour, and a few moments later returned with his very anxious wife. She offered to bring them ice tea, coffee, or perhaps a small glass of sherry, but Beatrix said they were not staying that long.

Horace waved her to a seat. "I, that is, we, apologize for arriving unannounced, but this is not a social call. It's more of a religious nature. You see, I had no idea you were so interested in the Episcopal Church."

"What?" they blurted in unison.

"Yes, the Episcopal Church. You see, if I had known your interest I would have gladly loaned you a copy of the Prayer Book, but I would like you to return my copy." He pointed to a small black leather book on a side table. "I believe it's the one you took from my room. It's the old outdated one version, but it was given to me by Bishop Whipple, and has sentimental value. He gave it to me, well, to my parents to give to me, when I was baptized. I'll be happy to buy you a copy of the new Prayer Book, if you would like one."

He watched as the color drained from Mrs. Melden's face, and she started shaking.

"You see, I believe you came into town this morning and stopped by the hotel when you were certain we were gone. I believe the timing was was intentional on your part."

"How did ... ?" she asked, handing him his book.

"How did I know it was you? For that, you can thank Doctor Howell here. She pointed out that there was a missing piece in this morning's activities. Let's review: You see, there were the four of us — Doctor Howell, my brother and I, and Fred my assistant. When we were surprised by the young man with the gun, the shotgun, your husband saved us from a very probable discomforting end. The assailant fired his gun which surely you must have heard since you live just next door. I'm sure of it, because it was loud enough to be heard across the river, so you obviously would have heard it if you were here. In fact, it was heard across the river. My sister-in-law heard the shot.

"What surprises me is that you did not come to see what was wrong, or whether your husband was alive, or injured, or dead. That's very odd. Again, surely, you must have heard the gun go off. Well, if you had been at home you would have heard it, except you were, as I just said, in the hotel going through my room and stealing my Prayer Book. You were inside the building, so you did not hear it. That means you are the missing piece. Oh, and thank you for the safe return of the book." Doctor Horace held out his hand, waiting for her to give it to him.

Beatrix instantly understood and added. "It is not the book you were looking for, is it?" She didn't wait for an answer. "No, it is not. You were looking for a book belonging to Miss LeBeau. Three books, to be more precise. One is a painter's recipe book; the other two are her diaries. You knew that they must be somewhere, and that they were not in the wardrobe, or upstairs in her bedroom. So, you assumed we had found them. On that point, you are quite right. We found them and took them for safe-keeping. You may trust me, when I tell you they are safe and secure."

She gasped in fear. "Have you read them?" she barely whispered.

Beatrix smiled. "Yes. The recipe book, I believe belonged to Vincent van Gogh. The diaries belonged to your late neighbor, and are also most fascinating."

Mrs. Melden put her head in her hands and started crying. "I was hoping to find them and burn them before anyone else could get them."

"I am sure you were hoping to procure them, although I question your intent to burn them. They are far too valuable for that. It may surprise you but I believe you are telling the truth when you say you wanted to find them, but for different reasons.. And fortunately, we got them first. The recipe for the van Gogh green alone is priceless," Beatrix said flatly. "It is also very dangerous."

"No! It's not that. We were never interested in the money. She had so many secrets that should never be told. Never!" she wailed. "If it ever gets out, people ..." Her voice trailed off.

"Which is why you looked through the wardrobe in the parlor, isn't it?"

"How do you know?" she sobbed.

"Because some of the jars were on the wrong shelf. Miss LeBeau had them meticulously organized, albeit very incorrectly. You or your husband must have moved them. You moved a bottle of cobalt to the shelf that only contained poisons."

"You knew we were here and were afraid we would eventually find them," Horace continued. "And so earlier today you slipped into town, waited for us to leave the hotel, and found out from the desk clerk we were gone for the morning. That would give you more than sufficient time. You told him you had been sent to retrieve something from my room, and you went up and looked for the diaries. You had plenty of time, but you were in a hurry, not wanting the chambermaid to catch you, and took my Prayer Book by mistake because you didn't take time to look at it. Understandable, but that was your fatal error. I'd hid it, but not too well. As I said, you were absent from your home this morning, so you are the only suspect. And my book on your table is sufficient evidence."

"There is little reason to deny it. I am quite sure the clerk can easily identify you, should it come to that," Beatrix added.

Horace and Beatrix sat quietly, carefully watching the terrified couple, allowing the news to sink into their minds. They were quite willing to wait for a response.

"Will she be arrested?" Mr. Melden asked.

"That is an interesting question," Doctor Horace said softly. "Lying to a desk clerk to gain unlawful entrance into a room might be considered a crime of gaining access to a room under false pretences. And then there is the matter of breaking and entering with intent. I'm not certain about stealing my Prayer Book; perhaps a felony, but more likely a misdemeanor."

"At the very least it would lead to further investigation," Beatrix added. "You might be charged as a co-conspirator with Miss LeBeau to fraud and forgery, and since you knew about the paint, or, the poison, and concealing evidence. That would be far more serious. Even if the charges were reduced, I can assure you an arrest and trial would be very unpleasant for both of you."

"I knew about the paint," Mrs. Melden said.

Horace and Beatrix remained silent, waiting for her to continue.

"One afternoon I came over to see if she needed anything from town since I was going in. I looked in through the front window. She had all those chemicals in that big wardrobe in the front parlour. I'd never seen it open before, but this time it was wide open. I saw her take out big bottles of yellow and green and go into the kitchen. I could see through to the back of the house from out in front on the porch, and she poured the green liquid into a pot on the stove and mixed in small amounts of the yellow, stirring it. I knew it wasn't dinner she was cooking up." She paused, the desperation in her eyes. "Then she came back out and got a bottle of blue. A small bottle."

"Tell them the rest," her husband urged.

"While it was cooling …" Mrs. Melden said hesitantly. "While it was cooling, I saw her pour something, a pale green liquid, into a small glass and come into the front parlour. I knew what it was. Just then, she turned around and I knew she'd seen me snooping, so I knocked on the door as if I'd just come up the front steps. She invited me in and offered me a glass of what she called 'The Green Fairy.'"

"Mrs. Melden, there is no reason to be coy. I am very sure it was not the first time you had absinthe," Beatrix told her. "As Doctor Horace said, we have the diaries."

Their hostess started crying again. "No. No it wasn't."

The woman continue sobbing. Mr. Melden, reached out to comfort her. "The two of them, they had it pretty much every day. I could always tell when they were into the stuff. It wasn't just the smell on her breath. It made her light headed, goofy, pretty strange. She's start seeing and imagining things."

Horace suddenly stood up, his right arm pressed tightly against his mid-section, doubling him up, loudly moaning in considerable pain. "Beatrix, we need to go back to the hotel. Now! Tell Fred to start the car," he gasped and winced.

She looked at him in alarm, and jumped to her feet to steady him. "Let me help you out to the car." The two of them shuffled and staggered a bit as they went down the stairs, and she held him tightly while he panted for air.

"Fred. Hotel! Now! When we get there, go find Doctor Theodore and if you cannot find him, have the desk clerk telephone Doctor Landis to come to the Butler immediately."

The two of them helped Horace into the back seat, and he slumped against Beatrix. "Go!" Beatrix shouted at Fred. She felt him slump against her.

A MURDER OF CROWS

CHAPTER SIXTEEN

"You can slow down now, Fred, before you kill us all," Horace said, suddenly sitting upright and smiling broadly. "I'm perfectly fine."

"Horace Balfour! What? What is going on?" Beatrix cried out. "What are you up to?"

"I'm perfectly fine; always was. I needed to get us out of there, and I couldn't think of anything else to do. I'm sorry, both of you, but it was time to leave right then and there. Feigning illness was the only idea I had."

Beatrix stared at him, her mouth open, her eyes blazing.

"I assure you I am perfectly fine. It was a ruse to get out of there, nothing more. I couldn't tell you because I wanted your reaction to be natural. I'm very sorry, but we really had to leave right then. Thank you both for playing your part in getting us out of there just in the nick of time. Now, take your time and drive back to the hotel. We'll use the back entrance."

"Horace Balfour, you are enough to make a preacher cuss!" Beatrix said angrily. "For a moment I thought …" she didn't finish her sentence.

"And I've made a lot of preachers cuss over the years, probably a few bishops, as well. Trust me, I've got a better vocabulary of cuss words than a top sergeant. My guess is that 'thunderation' covers them all and keeps me from getting my face slapped."

A confused and furious Beatrix said nothing until they were crossing the swing bridge. "If Mrs. Melden took your Prayer Book, then where are the two diaries and van Gogh's notebook?"

Horace chuckled. "Fred, by any chance would you happen to know?"

"I got them right here, boss, in my coat pockets. Safe and secure, just like you told me."

"Hidden in plain sight the whole time, Irene," Horace told her.

"What?"

"We kept them. I didn't want them in the hotel safe because the clerk knows the combination, and there was no way to be certain he wouldn't snoop. Nights can get boring for a front desk clerk, and snooping is always a temptation. And frankly, if Mrs. Melden hadn't found my Prayer Book in my room, I wouldn't put it past her to have the moxey to ask for the diaries from the clerk. Then, we did another diversion at the bank in case we were being watched or a teller was too talkative, so Fred has had them with him ever since. Some day you must read up on your military history, Doctor Howell, especially Baden-Powell at the Battle of Ladysmith during the Boer War."

"That still does not explain anything!" Beatrix snapped.

"I can fill you in on Baden-Powell, Doctor Howell, if you like," Fred offered.

"Not now!" she snapped at him.

"Look, a few minutes ago Mrs. Melden was getting ahead of us. Clarice has read the diaries, or most of them, maybe all of them, by now. At least, I hope she has. But there hasn't been time for her to tell us what's in them. That meant that Mrs. Melden was about to get ahead of us."

"So?"

"So, we had to get the jump on them. If we'd stayed much longer, then we would not know whether or not it was the truth. Those two have been cagey ever since we met them. I can't, we can't, trust a word they're saying. That's why we had to leave and get back to the hotel and find out what else Miss LeBeau put in her diaries. Beatrix, you were the one not wanting information to get out. Well, it might have if we'd let her continue. Thunderation, woman! We don't even know the right questions to ask!"

Beatrix was livid. Her nostrils flared, her eyes narrow, and she broke forth with a vehement, "Thunderation!" and then laughed. "Why didn't you say anything? You had the books!"

"They're in French, remember. Well, I hate to admit it, but I can't read French!" Horace said softly. He caught his breath, thankful he hadn't added the final word of "either."

"The less you knew, the safer you were, even when that fellow had a gun aimed at us. Remember, he said he was in business with Miss LeBeau, so she might have told him about her secret recipe, but we don't know if she did or not. If she had let it slip, I doubt he was likely to shoot us as long as he thought we got to the books first. We'd have to be alive to give them to him. Frankly, I don't think he could have walked into the hotel to sweet-talk the desk clerk to turn them over, but he might have strong-armed him. By the way, Fred, please remember to bring in that pouch of money this time. It isn't safe leaving it in the trunk of the car."

"Say, that's a good idea, Doc," he said solemnly.

"And the paintings, please," Beatrix added.

"I take it you want the poison paint left where it is," Fred told them. They did.

"But the gunman did not ask for the books," Beatrix objected.

"Our Mr. Melden didn't give him enough time. He and his wife believed the books existed, and probably hoped they were still in the house. He knocked out the man with the gun, knowing that the police would come, and that we would have to go to the station. And with us out of the way, he hoped he could still get them first."

Beatrix gasped. "That explains why he was watching us from his front window. I see."

"So, what was that there Mrs. Melden doing at the hotel?" Fred asked.

"They were taking no chances. They weren't able to find the books, but they didn't know if they were still in the house or if we had them. Something like a process of elimination," Horace said. "More like covering their bets."

"And just why, Doctor Balfour, were you so certain she would go to your room, and not Doctor Theo's or mine, or Fred's room?"

"I'd love to tell you that it is because she recognized my natural leadership, but the truth is, we got lucky again. Meanwhile, I didn't want Mrs. Melden to talk too much until we knew what Miss LeBeau wrote, and I didn't want us to be in the dark. So, we had to take a powder and get out of there fast. I thought it was best to be certain what we're looking at."

"I am still not certain I approve of your methods, Horace," Beatrix said firmly.

"Then you're in good company. I don't always approve of my methods, either."

As they went in the back door of the hotel Horace said, "I think it's time to have Clarice read us a story. Beatrix, you don't have to be part of it if the information about the Péladan Gang bothers you …"

"No. Thank you. I will keep myself composed. And, Horace, again, they are not a criminal gang."

"Whatever you think is best," he said, not letting her finish and explain. "And thank you for playing your part so very well."

"There are times, Doctor Balfour, when you are a very unlikeable man."

"I've been told that before. Many times, in fact. It's part of my charm."

"Thunderation," she growled at him, then winked.

"Fred, the money pouch, remember?" Horace asked.

"Oh, I just wanted to be sure you got up the stairs nice and safe like," he fibbed. "About to go out and get it right now."

When Horace and Beatrix were alone she asked, "Just why did you pretend to be on death's doorstep? Was it really necessary?

"You want the truth? It was the first thing that came to mind. I'm hoping that the latter part of the diaries will give us the answers we need so we can …"

"You think it will direct us to the killer?" she asked.

"Yes. And, to find out if our Mr. Péladan is dead, if we're lucky."

"Let us hope so," she said warily.

For the next two hours Clarice slowly made her way through the second diary, reading out loud to the rest of them.

"She certainly met some interesting people besides van Gogh and his brother. Oh, you'll like this dear," she said to her husband. "Another Theo. And listen to this list: Degas, Gauguin, Sati, Valadon, Debussy, Whistler, and, of course, their ring-leader Péladan."

"For a chambermaid from the hinterland, she was certainly an opportunist," Theo added with a tinge of disgust in his voice. "A

A MURDER OF CROWS

bunch of degenerate absinthe swilling artists and long-hair musicians. And, all of them under the spell of this madman Péladan. Who is this mysterious Péladan fellow, anyway?"

Beatrix blew the air out of her cheeks, paused, and answered. "I explained part of it to Horace. He was a brilliant charlatan who used a very strange blend of religious heresy and drama to deceive gullible people. He liked playing with people, just like girls playing with their dolls or boys their toy soldiers. Only, these were real people, and it wasn't make-believe. All of them were used. Remember that Russian monk, Rasputin, that brought down the Romanovs and Russia? Well, if he had had the opportunity, Peledan would have been just as bad. The man was evil, and he destroyed lives and careers." She closed her eyes and sighed as if the strength had left or body. Or, as if she had exorcised something evil.

"All right, a certifiable nut who belonged in the padded rooms. But who is this 'M'?" Theo asked.

"The future Mrs. Melden," Horace said, lighting his pipe. He handed it to Beatrix "Peace pipe?"

"Peace," she said, taking a puff and handing his pipe back. "Do you know the killer now?"

"Yes, I think so," he said quietly. Horace stood up and stretched, then walked out the door of his room. The others sat in silence, perplexed. Finally, Beatrix said, "Theo, your brother could use you."

"So, you figured out the killer?" Theo asked.

"Yeah," Horace said firmly

"And?"

"And what?"

"Well, for starters, not what, but who? Who is it? Who killed Miss LeBeau."

"Well, for starters then, walk with me down to the Western Union office so I can send a telegram to someone."

"To whom?" Theo asked.

"I'll tell you later."

"That doesn't make sense, even for you," Theo said. "You keep too many secrets."

" Trust me on this; it does make sense. That young fellow with the shotgun didn't kill her. He's guilty of a lot of other things, but murder isn't one of them. We need to spring him from Garrison's lock up before something happens to him."

"If he didn't kill the old lady, what did he do? And while you're at it, you want to explain that monkey business with the shotgun?"

"Fraud, conspiracy to commit fraud, conspiracy to commit forgery, among other things. It's enough to send him to the big house for a long stretch. He was the runner, the go-between between Miss LeBeau's chemistry operation and art forgers. We've got the evidence up in Beatrix's room. And, I'm going to tell you something I don't want you telling anyone, especially Beatrix. My money is on those two paintings being absolute fakes. Better to let the feds handle him than some angry millionaire banker who paid good cash money for a forged painting. A couple of years in the penitentiary will be better than being taken for a ride and a bullet in the back of his head."

"You're serious, aren't you? Except for that part about bankers shooting someone. Gangsters do that, not bankers," Theo chuckled. "You think Miss LeBeau was a forger?"

"Bankers and gangsters, they're all one and the same as far as I'm concerned. And yes, I am serious, and about those paintings being fake, too. You coming?"

"And if he isn't the killer, then who is?" Theo asked as they made their way down Butler Street. Horace didn't answer.

It wasn't until they had reached Dominic's barbershop that Horace stopped and turned toward his brother. "Right now, I'm not sure who he is. We don't know a thing about him, or maybe her. Not so much as a name. And Theo, to tell you the truth, I'm not certain even the Meldens really know what's going on. All I know for sure is that gunman didn't poison the old lady, and he didn't stick three knives in her back."

The two men paused in the middle of the sidewalk. Horace turned to his brother, and with a finger pointing at him said, "Right now, I'm not proof-positive that the Meldens really are the Meldens. That could be a phony name, maybe a cover for something."

"What do you think, then?" Theo asked. He was confused and couldn't form the right words, much less a coherent sentence.

"The only thing I know for sure is we saw the deceased with three knives in her back, and that might not have been the real cause of death. Thunderation! Just when we thought we knew the answers, this comes up!"

"What comes up?" Theo asked.

"I wish I knew. I think it's the paintings. It doesn't make sense that Beatrix is certain they are by van Gogh, and yet, you heard her. She doesn't want to examine them," Horace said.

"She said she didn't want to examine them in any laboratory but her own, that's all." Theo objected.

"I don't think she wants to know the truth about them! And her reaction at the mention of Péladan; it's not right. Something is wrong." He stopped himself from saying he wondered if Beatrix still might be under his spell.

Theo thought it over, wondering if his brother was having some doubts about Beatrix. He decided not to mention it, but asked, "Well, do you even know who you're sending a telegram to?"

"Yup. That part I do know."

"And are you going to let me in on this deep dark secret?" he asked hotly.

"Nope. Not just yet. Right now, the less you know might be the safest — for you *and* Clarice. Fred and Beatrix, too. Maybe. Then again, maybe not. But until I get a handle on something solid, I'm protecting you, little brother, by keeping you in the dark."

Theo was angrily silent, knowing his brother would not reveal anything more. He waited outside the telegraph office, sitting on a bench, trying to make sense of it.

He didn't succeed. His brain was a jumble of ideas, and it sent a chill through him,

A MURDER OF CROWS

CHAPTER SEVENTEEN

"I think the Meldens will be a lot more open about talking with us this morning," Horace said calmly as he, Theo, and Beatrix waited for Fred to bring up the car.

"Why might that be?" Beatrix asked.

"I doubt they had a very restful night. They know their world is collapsing around them. By now they are tired and will need to talk. I'm sure of it."

"And you? Did you have a restful night?" she asked.

"Absolutely."

"Think they'll tell us the truth?" his brother asked.

"Now, that's always the question, isn't it?"

"We haven't slept," Mr. Melden apologized for his appearance.

"I understand," Horace said. He glanced over at Theo as if to say 'I told you so.'

"I s'pose you've come to arrest us," Mr. Melden said quietly.

"We'll talk about that later," Theo said firmly.

They were invited to sit in the front parlor, and after some long uncomfortable coughing, Horace began. "Let's come straight to the point. You already know we have the diaries as well as van Gogh's book. Mrs. Melden, I believe you were telling us the gospel truth when you said you were trying to find them, and that you weren't doing it for money. You wanted to keep your own secrets hidden. I'm convinced of that from what we read."

"Thank you," she said quietly.

"We may be wrong, but I believe you were also doing it to protect her, perhaps to protect her memory, although for the life of me, I can't understand why you would even bother taking such risks. I'm not sure she was worth it," Horace told her.

No one responded to his uncomfortable words, and Beatrix's eyebrows arched.

Beatrix broke the silence. "Since you have not yet seen the diaries, you did not know what was in them. So, one of you, Mr. Melden or Mrs. Melden, or both of you, you also wanted to protect your own reputations, especially yours, Mrs. Melden. Now, that is very, very understandable. All the same, I agree with Doctor Balfour, I am not sure she was worth protecting. She was not a nice person."

"I guess none of that matters much any more," Mr. Melden said. "Our reputations, that is, will be ruined. It'll probably all come out in court."

Horace grimaced slightly, thinking that if the old man was fishing for them to give some answers, he wasn't going to get very far. Nor was he going to get a sympathetic hearing.

"There is something I don't understand. There is a note in Miss LeBeau's diary from August 1890, that she met 'M' for the first time. Is that 'M' for Marie?"

"Yes," Mrs. Melden said quietly.

"What I want to know is how you met," Beatrix interrupted. "You are not French."

Mrs. Melden let out a long sigh. "No, but my mother was. I grew up in Rhode Island and I graduated from Smith, the woman's college, perhaps you have heard of it. After that, I wanted to go on the grand tour. All the girls were doing it back then. Some of them went to England in search of a husband with a title. Well, they would have settled for a knight if it meant they could be called 'Lady So and So,' but I went to Paris. I wanted to see the City of Lights, meet writers and artists, and, well, this sounds pathetically silly now, I wanted to be one. I soon discovered I never had any real talent.

"I had a small apartment in St. Germain, but all the artists were all living up in Montmartre. It was dreadful there. Terrible poverty, the smells, the noise — yelling and screaming, cursing in all sorts of languages, arguing day and night. But at night, they would go to the cafes and taverns. They were absolute dives. I went, too, and I met more of them. That's where I met Catherine. She had moved from Auvere-sur-Oise where she knew the van Gogh brothers, and she said she met Gauguin. Maybe she did, maybe not. I don't know. She could talk a good story, and she dreamt of being their muse, a model, a mistress to an artist or writer. I'm ashamed to say it to any artist or writer. She practically threw herself at them. It's horrible to say that about her, but it is the truth.

"I felt so innocent and so naive, and she seemed so worldly. We became friends, and we became friends with Degas the artist and Satie the musician, and I can't remember all of the rest. There were so many of them. Oh, and Suzanne Valadon, the artist. Catherine modelled for her a few times." Mrs. Melden paused again, then said very softly, her head down, "So did I. It was in the all together, if you understand my meaning."

"I see," Beatrix said. "I believe it is called figure studies now."

"We drank wine and danced with men, and she gave me my first drink of absinthe. It must have gone to my head because I began hearing colors and seeing music. Weird wonderful dreams, and somehow, I can't remember how, but after a while we became part of Joséphin Péladan's circle.

"We would drink absinthe and wine and smoke opium, and then he would lead us in these strange rituals he promised would take us back in time. Back in time so we could experience true spiritual religion …" Mrs. Melden pause, remembering.

"It was madness really. Utter madness. Play-acting and decadence. He, Péladan, that is, taught us that decadence should be honored and worshipped as a way of breaking free of our inhibitions. I knew it was wickedly wrong, against everything in my upbringing, and would destroy me, but I was so addicted to it.

"And then one day I came to my senses. I knew I had to get out of there. I had to leave before I ended up in a cemetery, and I did. Leave, that is."

"How in the world did you end up here?" Theo asked.

"It is a long story. It's neither here nor there, but when I came here, to the States, I didn't go back home. I moved to New York and then Chicago, and finally here. I decided I wanted to get as far from a city as possible! I wrote to Catherine and I begged her to come over. I bought her a third-class ticket on a boat. They were cheap then. Steerage was, back then. And I paid for her train ticket to come to Chicago, and then I brought her up here. She told me she would pay me back a hundred times over. Now, I wish I had never done it. Ever! I tried rescuing her from all that decadence and what Péladan was doing, but I ended up bringing evil to my own doorstep." She took a deep breath, then paused, her face drawn.

"Poor Caroline Catherine. She had been modelling for Valadon and some others, like I said, but she was insanely in love with Erik Satie. Valadon had had an affair with him, then threw him over. That's when Catherine wanted to be introduced to him, and Valadon laughed at her. Laughed! What would he want with a peasant girl like her, a peasant girl from the country? Péladan was just as bad. The two of them laughed at her? Even if it was true, it was such a cruel thing to say. It crushed her spirits. I think she would have thrown herself in the Seine if it hadn't been for my letter."

Mrs. Meldon looked up, fury in her face. "I wish she had taken her life! There! I've said it. After all these years keeping it to myself, I can say I wish she had died long ago!

"Well, she came, and for a while she was better. She showed me this little notebook she had. It had little dabs of color and instructions how to make them. She said van Gogh had given it to her, but I didn't believe her. Not at first, anyways. We spent our days with some of the local artists, and tried to become painters. Then, one day we went for a walk along the river, and she just stared at the trees and the bushes and kept talking about the green and she knew how to make a green paint that was more beautiful than anyone had ever seen."

" Van Gogh's green?" Theo asked.

"Yes! She had these two rolled up paintings of wheat fields that she showed me, and said she knew the secret to making his green, and how we would be rich beyond imagination, only we couldn't tell anyone.

"For a few years she was normal as you or me. She worked as a chambermaid in town, and in some of the shops, and kept to herself. Her English wasn't very good, and she didn't mix in very well. Both of us were like that, saving our money to buy nice clothes and marry a good man and have a nice house. I did. but she didn't. She didn't have it in her, the drive and determination. Instead, it was the Green Fairy. Always the Green Fairy. You know the story of the genie in a bottle that makes your wishes come true? Well, her genie came out of the bottle and wrapped his hands around her throat like the devil and it addled her mind. It got to the point if there was good news, the Green Fairy helped her celebrate; and if there was bad news, then she drowned her sorrows in it. All the time!

"I could hear her singing at night the old songs from Paris and I knew the Green Fairy had her. After a few years she went mad. Look at her place! No sane woman plants poison around her house and does the things she did. She started making her own green fairy. She had to, once it was outlawed. That's what that little apothecary still was for — to get the oil of wormwood and fennel. I sipped it once, just once, and I knew, I just knew, what was addling her brain. It didn't taste right, and it wasn't the Green Fairy anymore — it was the green devil. You think the devil wears red. No, for her it was green."

"And the van Gogh green?" Horace asked, pressing the point.

"She learned to make it. A perfect match, wet or dry. It's easy to match it wet or dry, but nearly impossible to do it both ways. And she did!"

"It is laden with poison — arsenic, cadmium, cobalt," Beatrix said.

"She told me it was Paris Green and cadmium yellow, along with some other things," Mrs. Melden replied. She lowered her eyes, "I don't think she trusted me with how to make it."

"Paris Green is arsenic, cadmium is just as dangerous. For that matter, so is cobalt and the copper acetate we found. And you say you saw her cooking it over the stove?" Beatrix asked.

"Yes, once." She paused. "Well, maybe more than that. At first she would make just a tiny amount, a few ounces. Just for herself. But the past year or so …"

"Pints and quarts. And she would sell it to that man with the gun?" Horace asked.

"Yes," Mr. Melden answered. "But he wasn't the first. There was another man who came at first. I knew he was up to no good from the get-go."

"Let me ask you a question, Mr. Melden. When were you in the Army?" Theo asked, interrupting his brother and Beatrix.

"Spanish American War, like I said, only it was the Marines in the Philippines, not Cuba. And let me tell you, that was brutal. The malaria and the insurrectionists. Brutal," he answered. "Mrs. Melden and me married after I got my discharge papers."

Theo smiled. "I thought as much."

Horace became serious. "Now, I will tell you what I am certain happened. You were both aware of Miss LeBeau's increasing insanity, and you knew the reason for it. You tried to take care of her and protect her, but you were increasingly helpless, weren't you? It kept getting worse and worse these last months, didn't it? Between the absinthe, your green fairy as you call it, and making the green paint.

"You may find some comfort when I tell you, and my brother and Doctor Howell will agree with this: there was nothing you could have done to save her. By then, it was far too late. Years, too late. The wormwood in the absinthe, all of the poison around the house — just the pollen from the hemlock alone, and the arsenic and cadmium, were responsible. Not just handling the chemicals, but she was inhaling it when she was mixing it. It was well beyond your control. You must understand, she brought this on herself. Do I make myself clear?"

"Yes," both of them barely whispered.

"I believe, Mrs. Melden, you found her on the floor, in contortions, probably unconscious and near death. You had never seen anything so hideous and frightening. You ran back home for you to help, and then and you Mr. Melden went back together. When you saw her in that condition you did what every sailor, soldier, and marine would have done when they saw a comrade mortally wounded. You ended the suffering rather than letting it continue.

"Some would say it is morally wrong, that it is murder. I don't know, maybe it is, I just don't know. What I do know is when I was in a field hospital in France, there were men who were crying for their mothers and men who were begging for someone to kill them, the pain was so great.

"After you had done it, you were surprised that you couldn't pull out the knife. Her muscles were already cramping up, and they tightened around the blade. Think back to your basic training, man, and hand to hand combat. Sometimes a soldier has to fire his rifle to pull out his bayonet. Or, you have enough leverage with the rifle to pull out the blade. But you were working with a short knife. I believe you told your wife, and for a moment she remembered Péladan and his strange rituals involving three daggers. One of you found two more knives. You made it look like some sort of satanic ritual, and you carefully removed any fingerprints. Perhaps it was a ritual, perhaps to exorcise your own personal devil, or something else. I don't know and I don't need to know. At least not right now."

Beatrix interrupted. "There is something you must know, and listen carefully to understand this: I am not certain you even killed her. You may have been seconds too early or too late, no more or less than that. There was very little blood from the wounds. Her heart had either stopped or was barely beating by then. Even with all my training as a forensic pathologist, I would have no way of knowing one way or the other even if I were at the finest laboratory in the nation, or the world."

"That's a relief," he said with a deep sigh. "I didn't mind going to prison if I was found guilty, but I didn't want to spend eternity in hell." He reached over to hold his wife's hands, both of them wanly smiling.

"So, that's that," Horace said. "We know what happened, and how it happened."

Mr. Melden stood up to shake his hand.

"We're not done yet. Please sit back down," Horace said, pointing to the chair. "There's a lot of unfinished business. First, we found the last of her paint, and it is going to be destroyed. It is too dangerous to be used. Just opening the jars is lethal. Is that understood? There is no more van Gogh green, and there will never be any more. Ever!"

Both of them nodded, and Horace hoped Beatrix would not start explaining the economic ramifications of duplicating the paint. She didn't.

"There is also the matter of two van Gogh paintings in the upstairs of her house. The wheat fields, you first saw years ago, Mrs. Melden."

"There is no way you can be allowed keep them. They don't belong to you, and I think you know that. There is no clear line of ownership. Perhaps van Gogh gave them to her; perhaps the owner of the hotel did so; maybe van Gogh's brother, or maybe she stole them. The point is, there is no clear line of ownership. I know this is disappointing to you, I am telling you this for your own good. As you may already know, they are worth a fortune, several thousand dollars each, but if you tried selling them, you would implicate yourselves in this sordid business, and no amount of money is worth that," Beatrix said.

"That much money?" Mrs. Melden gasped, instinctively putting her right hand over her mouth.

"And all of that depends on whether they are genuine or very good fakes," Horace added. He looked at Doctor Howell, but there was no change in her expression.

Beatrix waited to see if the couple would object. They didn't say anything, but their disappointment was obvious. "In that case, I can make arrangements for them to be delivered as an anonymous gift to an art museum. There will be questions and inquiries, but you will be kept far out of it. It really is for the best."

"And first they will have to be authenticated. Is that clear?" Horace asked.

The couple silently nodded in agreement.

"There is some happier news in all of this," Beatrix continued. "It is the matter of a leather pouch that Fred found the other day when he was looking for the paint. I believe that odious man with the shotgun was in search of it. It does not belong to us, so it is not ours to keep. There is no point in involving Chief Garrison. Frankly, I do not believe the man would know what to do. So, we three are in agreement that you are to keep the money to use as you see fit. It is not a reward for what you did that night, but what I believe is just payment for your years of caring for Miss LeBeau. Fred, the pouch." She watched as Fred handed it to Mr. Melden. The couple were speechless.

Fred blew the air out of his cheeks and cocked his head to one side. "Now, I've been studying up on this situation you done did get into, and you know, after all you've been through for all these years, and now living next to a house where your neighbor was murdered, I just can't imagine you two wanting to stay here. Now, if it were me and my missus, that is if I had one, which I don't, then I'd be telling everyone all over the place about not wanting to live next to a murder site, and we'd be selling up quickie-like and move far away. You get my drift?"

Mr. Melden thought for a few seconds. "My brother, he's dead now, but his son has a place down near Cairo in Illinois …"

"Fred is right. That looks to me like a very good idea," Theo said. "Winter's coming on, so I wouldn't waste any time. Not a single day."

"So, I believe that wraps up everything," Horace said. "I'm sure you two have lots to discuss." He stood, Theo and Beatrix joining him, as Fred led the way out to the car.

Mrs. Melden came out after them to thank them, then asked, "And the diary? What about the diary?"

Beatrix gave her a rare smile and said, "Yes," It was an answer without information.

"You were a bit quick off the mark handing over the loot," Horace told Beatrix when they were back in the car. "Perhaps," she replied. "But none of us need it, and it would not be right to keep it. To give it to the chief would only confuse the man. It is a considerable amount, and perhaps just might corrupt him. Logically, the best place for it was with them. They have a chance to start a new life and a reasonable and holy hope for happiness. I believe that is something all of us want. We made it possible for them to have a second chance," Beatrix said firmly.

Horace nodded in agreement.

A MURDER OF CROWS

CHAPTER EIGHTEEN

"So, that's the end of that. Well, except for figuring out what we're going to tell the police chief," Theo said quietly, once they returned to the hotel and sat on the front porch chairs.

"Not hardly, if only we were that lucky," Horace answered back. "We know how Miss LeBeau died, we know potentially who had a hand in her passing and desecrated the corpse, and why. About the only thing that's settled is the money. We're not nearly done." He turned to Beatrix, "So, what do we do about the two paintings, the poison paint, and the diary, Doctor?"

She shook her head. "I don't have a clear idea. It is a true challenge. Well, perhaps getting rid of the paint will not be all that difficult. I suggest we talk to the pharmacist. Undoubtedly, he would know the best place to dispose of it, and I am sure he will be discreet and careful."

"One down, two to go," Theo said, then added, "maybe."

"The paintings are a challenge. Horace, Theo; I do not know if they are genuine van Gogh pieces or not. As I said the other day, I would need to examine them very carefully, and the truth of the matter is, I do not know that I want to do it."

"Why?" Horace asked, surprised.

"If they are copies or fakes, there is not a problem. It would almost be a relief. If they are genuine, there will be questions about legal ownership. We certainly do not own them. In fact, right now, a good case could be made that we stole them."

"Too bad one of the Meldens didn't run upstairs and liberate them," Fred said. "At least they could say the dead lady gave them to her."

"That is very true. There would not be a paper trail of ownership, but it would be their word against anyone else. Perhaps. However, if they are genuine, it is entirely possible the French might want them back as part of their national heritage, so one way or another there would likely be lawsuits."

"What makes the Frenchies think they have any right to them?" Fred demanded. "They didn't care two raps about him when he was alive, so why should they get grabby now that he's dead?"

"Fred, I understand what you are saying, but you must believe me, that is how things fall out sometimes," Beatrix told him. "There is even good reason to believe the Dutch might get into the mess and claim them since van Gogh was Dutch."

"So?" Horace asked.

"The only idea that comes to mind right now is I know a young man at the art museum in Chicago. I worked with him in the past, and I believe he is both competent and discreet. If, and it is a very big "if," I took the paintings to him and told him I am in the middle of a donation from an anonymous source, he might make himself useful. I would need to talk with him first, and in hypothetical terms, of course. It is a considerable risk for him."

"And, he'd believe the story?" Theo asked.

"Absolutely not. I said he was competent and discreet, not a fool. However, I would tell him once he received the canvasses he could not ask any questions. It would be up to him to examine them. I am sure others would take it from there."

"And that will work?" Theo asked her.

"I do not know. However, he is young, and one way to advance his career would be for him to get his hands on two unknown masterpieces. And then, we would have to hope that no one further up the line gets too curious about where it came from or has too many scruples," she said quietly.

Horace chuckled, "Or mind shattering the Ninth Commandment."

"How's that?" his brother asked.

"The one on coveting the neighbor's possessions. Let's just hope that they are fakes, and that will be the end of it. I'll tell you what bothers me about all of this, Beatrix. You won't get any recognition for having discovered them. Forget the morality angle. You'll be reduced to an intermediary," Horace said softly.

"More like a bag man for the Outfit," Fred sniffed in disdain. "Bad woman," he corrected himself.

"For which I will be grateful," Beatrix replied. "Look, it is going to take months, perhaps a couple of years, for someone to determine if the paintings are genuine and then have them appraised by someone else. After that there will be debates and committee meetings. Forensics, curators, experts, all of them going at it hammer and tongs. And it will not be the truth they are seeking as much as demonstrating their knowledge. No thank you. I will be happy to stay far away from it."

"Aren't you curious?" Fred asked.

Beatrix smiled. "Of course I am, but this is one time I want to stay far away from it. Trust me, gentlemen, it will be for the best. I will happily remain on the fringes and let someone else deal with it."

Horace started to reach out his hand to console her, but thought better of the gesture. "I'm sorry it turned out this way."

"Oh, do not be! I have been playing Irene to your Sherlock for some time. Now, I am going to have the role of Mycroft! The smarter brother who worked behind the scenes," Beatrix smiled.

"Thunderation!" Horace growled softly.

"What are you two going on about now?" Fred asked.

"I'll explain later," Horace told him. "So, that leaves the diaries and van Gogh's recipe book. What happens to them?"

"Well, the recipe book can go to the art museum with the two paintings. If anything, it might help prove whether or not they are genuine," Beatrix said. She laughed. "That book alone will keep the research department in full employment for years!"

"It's no good," Fred said.

"Why? Why ever not?" she asked.

"Well, Doc, on account of the fact that you done did tell us that the formula for his fancy green paint is in there. And, that's the stuff that caused this mess. Now, if you go telling the world about how to make it, then a whole lot of folks are going to try doing it and get themselves killed in the process. Sorry, Doc, but you'd better think that one through a bit more," Fred told the group.

"I have to admit it, but Fred's right," Horace said.

Beatrix looked at the three men. "There is a simple solution. Horace, you have a pen knife?" she said firmly.

"Yeah, and I can see where this is leading. But if we cut that part out and we, say, burn it, no one will ever know how he did it," Horace said. "Somehow that doesn't seem right."

"Giving them a recipe on how to make poison paint in the kitchen is not right, either. No, it is far better for the world to not have that formula. I shudder to think how dangerous it would be," Beatrix said firmly. "I believe van Gogh's formula should remain a secret, unique unto him alone. A secret he took to the grave."

"Besides, you've already memorized it," Theo told her.

"Yes, of course," she said with a sly smile.

He was tempted to say something, but a glare from Horace stopped him.

"So, now what?" Horace asked. "That leaves the diaries."

"I have an idea that might work. I know a woman who works in the acquisitions department at the Smithsonian. We're not friends, but I have seen her work, and I know her reputation. I could send her a letter and tell her that I am sending two diaries that are to stay locked away for fifty, maybe seventy five years. Locked and unopened because they have confidential information that should not be released due to their sensitive nature …" Beatrix said.

"And they would stay that way?" Theo asked.

"I am quite sure they would. They have a repository for other documents."

"Sure you don't mean depository?" Horace asked.

"Perhaps, but repository works in this case. They will be in repose for decades," she laughed at her own pun.

"Well, make it fifty, would you? That way, Phoebe will still be around when the story is told. I figure she deserves it, since she and her murder of crows got us into this mess," Horace suggested. "Fifty years is long enough. Anyone alive when the van Gogh boys were around will be pushing up daisies by then."

Beatrix silently nodded in agreement, finally saying, "Fifty it is."

"Well, that sort of wraps it all up, doesn't it?" Theo asked.

"Nosireebob! We gotta figure out what to tell the high and mighty Chief Garrison!" Fred said. Theo, Horace, and Beatrix stared at him, knowing he was right, and knowing there were no easy answers.

"I forgot about him," Horace groaned.

"I have been trying to forget about him since the first time I met him," Beatrix added.

CHAPTER NINETEEN

"The chief's going to be a real problem," Horace agreed. "Especially after he loses his prime suspect. Thunderation!" He winced in exhaustion and frustration.

He pulled out his pipe, knocked the dottle out of it, packed it, and lit it. "Unless you have a spare cigar in your pocket … ?" Beatrix asked, holding out her hand. He didn't, but handed her his pipe. She took a long drag on it, leaned back her head, and slowly blew out the smoke.

"There's something unsettling about a woman smoking a pipe," Theo said in disgust, watching her take a second drag before handing it back to Horace.

"I believe you also find it unsettling to see a woman have a bump from your hip flask, although you have often been very generous. And if you are offering …" Beatrix held out her hand, amused at Theo's discomfort as he handed it to her.

"Go on and finish it up, Sister. I mean, begging your pardon, Doctor, I got plenty more up in the room to refill it," Fred said. Theo glared at him, miffed at what he considered a lack of decorum.

"In that case," she smiled, then drained it. "Thank you."

"I won't be surprised to hear you've become a flapper," Theo growled.

"All right, let's all settle down and figure this out. We've broken so many laws the past few days, the way things are going I won't be surprised if we end up as the chief's guests," Horace sighed. "The floor is open to reasonable ideas to avoid that."

No one said anything. Horace and Theo were looking at their feet; Beatrix staring off across the Kalamazoo River.

"It's a dilly of a pickle, isn't it?" Theo asked. "The chief might have the wrong man locked up for murder, and if he has to let him go, he'll go after the Meldens. Neither of them killed Miss LeBeau, but they've done plenty to get themselves right into the soup. And let's face it, we stole the paintings and diaries. I don't care how good the reasons, or noble the cause, it's still theft, and I don't think the chief is bright enough to say otherwise."

"Don't forget giving away a bag full of money that wasn't ours rightfully to give to them," Fred added.

They lapsed into silence again.

Horace sat up, his eyes blazing. "All right. Beatrix, you've got to get out of town this afternoon. I'll have Fred take you up to the train station. Theo, tell Clarice she has to go with Beatrix to Chicago. There's a train in a couple of hours that will take you into Union Station. From there you two go by taxi to the Palmer House and stay there. Tomorrow morning, take the paintings and get rid of them. Sound reasonable?"

"It sounds more like you are trying to keep us out of harm's way," she retorted.

"Not exactly, but yes, sort of, after a fashion. You two can handle yourselves all right in Chicago. It's getting the paintings out of here that's important, and since you have the contact, you have to do it. We need to get them out of here before Garrison starts asking too many questions, and the only way to be sure they get delivered is for you to take them in person."

"I see," she said quietly.

"You know the people you need to see in Chicago. So …" Horace said firmly, repeating the plan.

"All right, I agree. Yes, it makes sense," she finally admitted. "We can save the paintings. That is important."

"And I hope you like shopping," Theo added. "I doubt Clarice can go to Chicago without stopping at Marshall Fields and the Carson store."

"Well, get moving," Horace encouraged her.

"And what if the chief wants to know where we are?" she asked.

"We'll just say you went into Chicago to do some shopping. He'll drop that topic right then and there. If we have to, we'll tell him for ladies' under-things," Theo said. "And keep an eye onClarice. Don't let her spend too much. And, stay together!"

Twenty minutes later Clarice and Beatrix were packed and ready to leave. Fred had the car in front of the hotel, waiting for them. "Where are the paintings?" Horace asked.

"Out of their frames, off the stretchers and rolled up," Beatrix answered. "Fred will see to it that the wood is burned to get rid of the evidence. The paintings are in my bag. We divided things up in case. Clarice has the diaries in case we run into trouble. For modesty's sake I prefer not to disclose the location of the formula book," Beatrix said. She paused to look at Horace and quietly said, "Tell me that you know what you are doing, please."

"All I know is that getting those things out of here seems wise," Horace said firmly. He didn't add that he wanted her out of town, too.

Beatrix smiled. "Clarice said something about how we are taking it on the lamb and ditching the evidence and getting put on ice for a while. I am not certain what she meant by that, and I cannot help wonder if she has done this before."

"You'll have to ask her, but I doubt it," Theo said. "Probably, some lingo she picked up."

"Time for a quick hug and a kiss," Clarice told her husband, forcing a smile. "I'll be worried the whole time about you." She wrapped her arms around his waist and gave him a kiss. Horace and Beatrix waited awkwardly, finally shaking hands.

"Boss, you want me to drop them off and come back here right away?" Fred asked.

"No! Here's the plan: Go to the station and then you go in and get two tickets to Chicago. Have the ladies stay in the car while you get them. And then take them for a little sight-seeing until it's time for them to get on the train. About ten minutes before it's due into the station should be right. With luck, you won't have any company, but watch your back. After that, go stop and see your friends at your hang-out for a while. If the chief wants to know where you are, I'll tell him you went to get a haircut."

"Got it, General," Fred said, snapping a salute in Horace's direction. He opened the car doors for the two women, then put the luggage in the trunk. "Say, Doc, what if the chief is watching the station? Then what?"

"Good thinking. The next stop is in Fennville. If you think you're being watched, pull out of the station nice and slow and then get down to Fennville. I doubt you'll be tailed, but watch out."

"Consider it done!" Fred smiled.

Beatrix opened the window and motioned for Horace to come closer. To his surprise, she said, "Don't let anything happen to you. Promise?"

He nodded in agreement. "You, either. Promise?"

"I'm not fond of that woman," Theo said as Fred pulled away, "but I think you could have been a little, well, warmer. You could have said goodbye a little better, you know."

"That didn't occur to me," Horace said, watching the car pull away.

"You know, and I'm sorry to say it, but I do believe you, big brother, I do believe you." Theo reached up to clap Horace on the shoulder. "Now what?"

Horace blew the air out of his cheeks. "Well, the hotel dining room is still open. Something to eat seems like a good idea. We'll think better."

"Let's hope so."

After their late lunch the brothers moved back to the porch rocking chairs and Horace pulled out his pipe. "You mind switching places with me?" Theo asked. "I swear, it smells like you're burning your old socks in that thing." They got up and exchanged places.

"You come up with an idea?" Theo asked.

"Yeah. We let Garrison make the next move. He's going to ask where the ladies are, and like I said, we'll tell him they went to do a bit of shopping . That should stop him quick enough. And if he asks where Fred is, we tell him he went up to Holland to get his hair cut and see some old army buddies."

"You already said that. And if Garrison still wants to know where the women are, then what?"

"We'll act surprised that they conspired with Fred to go up to the station to take the train into Chicago."

"He might ask where they're staying? Or, when they are coming back? Then what?"

Horace chuckled. "Oh, you know Fred. We can count on him to have a case of forgetfulness about what a couple of women were chatting about. If it comes to that, which I doubt. Besides, Garrison might not even ask about them."

"Fine, just fine," Theo said sarcastically. "And what about springing that fellow from the jail? I'm guessing that had something to do with the telegram you sent yesterday."

"It did," Horace said quietly.

"And?" Theo asked.

"We'll wait and see and let nature take its course."

"There are times, Horace, when you are the most infuriating man in the world!"

"I've heard that on more than one occasion. Look, I don't know exactly how this is all going to play out, and trying to second guess what might or might not happen isn't going to get us too far. Not now, anyway. Besides, I've got more important things to think about."

"More important? Such as?" Theo demanded, his voice rising in anger.

"Well, I have to figure out how to explain to Phoebe about her dead crows, and Harriet will have talked to her principal, so I have to figure out what to say if they want me to talk."

"Crows! At a time like this you're worried about what to tell a bunch of school children about some dead crows."

"Worry is not a word I use. I'm thinking. Of course, if you'd like to talk to them about what killed them, then you do the thinking and I'll close my eyes for a while and take a nap." Horace said quietly, resting his hands over his abdomen.

"Not so fast," Theo shot back at him. "That business about why Melden said he put three knives in the old lady's back. That got a bit creative, don't you think?"

"I'm not certain I did. Maybe it was to put Garrison and us on the wrong trail. Then, when you take into account what Mrs. Melden and Beatrix both said about Péladan, maybe they did it to make sure she was dead and stayed that way. You know, like driving a stake through the heart of a vampire," Horace said.

"Ah, that's pure bilge-water and you know it," Theo retorted. Horace didn't answer. He was breathing steadily, drifting off to sleep.

The two men sat in the afternoon sun, still warm for so late in the year, until Harriet and Phoebe came down the street and walked up the hotel front steps. Phoebe startled her grandfather with a hug, and he awoke with a start. She was bubbling with excitement. "Mother made all the arrangements for you to talk at the school assembly tomorrow morning!" She saw the puzzled look on his face, and reminded him it was about the dead crows.

Horace was about to answer when two cars pulled up in front of the hotel. He recognized the driver of one of them — the police chief. To their surprise, he got out of his car with a big smile on his face. "Stick around, would you?" he asked Harriet and Phoebe.

"I want you to meet a genuine agent from the Federal Bureau of Investigation, agent Orville Ryan," the chief said. "He's come to take my prisoner off my hands. Looks like he's wanted by the federal government, I'm proud to say. And proud to say I arrested him!"

Theo and Horace looked at each other. For the second time, they had done all the work and the chief was taking all the credit.

"Just thought you'd like to know I got this whole murder investigation wrapped up, and I spared the county the money of a trial to boot, what with the feds taking him off my hands." They watched as the agent got out of his car and waited for Theo and Horace to come down to the sidewalk.

"Doctors Balfour, a real pleasure to meet you. When the director received your telegram yesterday he wired our office and ordered us to get on to it right away. He thinks mighty highly of you two for all the service you've given to our country," Ryan said.

"Thank you," Theo said, still puzzled.

"Let's go for a walk. There are some things I want to talk over with you, just to get them straight for my report. I spend so much time behind a desk that I like to walk when I think. Chief Garrison, you will remain here."

Fred returned, much earlier than Horace or Theo had expected, and parked in front of the hotel. "There's police work going on here," Chief Garrison snapped at Fred as he got out of the car. "Until you get permission, you're staying put, right here. You can stay right there in the car."

"Say, what's going on?" Fred asked.

"I told you. Police work, and it isn't any of your business, so pipe down."

The three men slowly sauntered down Butler Street. "First of all, thank you for helping get our agent out of the jail!" Ryan said, then chuckled, "Your police chief is certain he had the right man. He missed that one by a country mile. Our agent has been watching Miss LeBeau the last few days after the agents in the Chicago office arrested her accomplice in Elgin. We'd been tailing that suspect for a while because we couldn't figure out why one man would buy so much arsenic. When they brought him in he said it was to kill rats. We finally got the real story out of him and he named names. Well, just one name: Miss LeBeau. The man you waylaid is one of ours."

"Sorry about the way he got roughed up," Horace said, wincing in embarrassment.

"Don't give it a second thought. He'll be a little bruised for a few more days, but you probably did him a big favour. It protected his identity. Word will get out that he was arrested and released, and that'll be a bonus on his next case. It will make it easier for him to work undercover. Now, the only thing left is to find out what happened to all that poison."

"Oh, we secured that for you, as well," Horace said.

"Really? Good work, men!"

"It's locked up in the trunk of our car," Theo answered.

"Good work, men!" he repeated.

"And if you go out to the LeBeau house you'll find plenty more. We just took the finished product. The rest of it is still raw materials," Horace added.

At the end of the second block they turned around and slowly sauntered back towards the hotel. "I'll be sure to mention your names in my report to the director's office, not that it will go any further than that, I'm sorry to say. I think you realize that if that poison had gotten into the wrong hands, and then into, say, a public water system, hundreds would have been killed."

"We're more than happy to be rid of that stuff," Theo said.

"One more thing. Let's keep our chief in the dark on all of this, shall we? The Bureau doesn't like to share all of its intelligence with outsiders. I'm sure you understand."

"And we'll be more than happy to do that!" Horace said.

"What he says goes double for me. You can count on it," Theo added.

It took only a few minutes for the three quarts of poison to be moved from the back of the car they'd rented to the agent's car. "I'd be real careful about not getting rear-ended," Fred advised. The agent said he would take that under advisement.

There were handshakes all around, a few final words, and the chief stood grinning in triumph as the agent drove off. Still in handcuffs was the prisoner, sitting in the back seat. "Yes, Sir! Captured a man wanted by the federal agents!" he announced to some guests coming down the front steps of the hotel.

"Now, I've got some questions for you two," the chief said.

"And they can wait. I have an important medical conference to attend," Horace said.

"Where?"

"Right here, with my granddaughter. There is still the matter of the dead crows," Horace said.

"Dead crows? Not that monkey shine business again."

"Right now, that is far more important than your questions. It shouldn't take too long. Just a few minutes."

The chief muttered something about going into the hotel restaurant for a cup off coffee. "Join me when you're done. I still got questions for you two."

"I think they've run out of donuts, if that's what you're looking for," Horace told him.

CHAPTER TWENTY

"So, Grandfather, can you speak at my assembly tomorrow? Mother and the principal said I could introduce you," Phoebe asked.

"No, I don't think I'm going to do it," he said thoughtfully.

"Why? You promised and it's all arranged!"

"Well, I've been thinking it over. I think you should give it. You did all the work. You observed the crows, and then like a real scientist you started asking questions. When people thought you were being foolish, you didn't quit. You persevered. That's what a scientist does. And, you asked more questions. You went right to the best person possible, Doctor Howell. You found the right answers because you worked at it."

"But Grandfather, you make it sound so simple!"

"No. It isn't simple. It was difficult at the time, and now that you have the answers, it only seems simple. Does that make sense?"

Phoebe thought about it for a few moments and said softly, "I guess so."

"Thunderation! I know so. You did some first rate work, and at an age much younger than your uncle or I. So, I think you should be the one to present a medical paper to your colleagues, not me!"

"But ..."

"Now, hear me out. You have all the information. The big task is to organize your thoughts. Begin with what you observed — something very unusual when you saw three crows fall from the sky. Tell them what you did, and how you went well beyond the ordinary by writing to Doctor Howell. Then tell them about your consultation with her and what she told you.

"After that, then tell your colleagues the danger of eating apple seeds because they contain cyanide which is a deadly poison. You can do that, can't you?"

"I think so," she said thoughtfully.

"I know so! And what's more, after you have given your report, I expect you to send a copy of it to me. I'm going to have my secretary type it up, and we'll send it to the medical association to be printed so other physicians around the country, maybe the world, will see it. You might be saving lives, you know."

"Really?" Her eyes widened in excitement.

"Yes, really. I'll tell you what, before we send it out, I'll write an introduction, but you get full credit for it. Jake with you?"

"Jake with me!" Phoebe and her grandfather spit into their left palm and slammed their right first into it.

"Phoebe!" her mother exploded. "That's disgusting!"

"Settle back, Harriet. It means we made a solemn promise and we're both going to keep our end of the bargain. You just have to see that she gets her paper written and mailed to me!"

Harriet looked around, then over both shoulders. She shuddered and whispered, "Oh well, here goes." She joined them in their secret pact. "Thunderation, that's disgusting," she said.

"But you will be there tomorrow, won't you?" Phoebe asked.

"Yes, but then we have a train to catch. I have to get back home, and your aunt Clarice and Doctor Howell have already left. So, as soon as the applause dies down, we have to say goodbye for a little while.

"Oh," she said softly, trying not to whimper.

"Well, I got it all figured out," the chief said when Horace and Theo joined him in the dining room. "You getting here so early, that FBI agent, and the murder.

"And just what did you figure out?" Theo asked.

"Well, that business about dead crows was just a smokescreen. I'm pretty sure of it now. I know a smokescreen when I see one, and that was a doozy. You pulled a fast one, but I caught on. You got down here so quicky-like because you'd already been instructed by the FBI that something wasn't on the up and up. That's how you got here all the way from Minnesota in what seemed like just a couple of hours instead of a day or so. You knew right from the get-go about the dead lady, maybe even before me, and about the poison, and that there was an accomplice just waiting to knock her off. And you brought in that lady doctor to help keep your cover, too. That was smart, because you almost had me convinced, but I saw through it right away!

"And then as soon as I had the murderer locked up, you sent a wire to your higher-ups. You had me fooled for a little while, but I'm kinda grateful to you for helping out."

"Only too happy to be of service," Theo said.

"I'd sorta kinda like you fellows to stick around another day or so," the chief said.

"Oh, I wish we could oblige, but we've been instructed to get down to Chicago tomorrow," Horace said.

"Bet something big going on. You want to let me in on the secret? Something to do with Capone and his henchmen? Yes, sir! That's what it is. Okay, I understand why you have to move on. Your next assignment. But give me a hint, would you?"

"Oh, I don't think we can do that," Horace said. "I'll tell you what you can do to help us. We've got get up to Holland tomorrow morning around 10 o'clock or so to get on the train. You want to give us a lift? It's sort of important, so maybe lights and sirens the whole way? It's not something I'd trust to anyone but you."

"Say, now that'll be a real honor," the chief said, a big smile on his face.

CHAPTER TWENTY ONE

Theo and Fred had seen it many times over the years. It was the way Horace contained himself right to the end, no matter what was going on in his mind and heart. That was assuming, of course, he had a heart. After she made her speech at the school assembly, he had congratulated Phoebe on her medical report, given her a long hug to say goodbye, given a hug to Harriet, and another to Phoebe, and left. It was only as he walked out of the school to the car when the energy seemed to drain out of him. It was far more than mere exhaustion. It was overwhelming sadness at saying goodbye.

"Come on, big brother, we'll be coming back in a few months," Theo said gently.

"I know, but she'll be older. What frightens me is that one day she is going to outgrow me. I realized that when I saw that young man carrying her books. We'll come down here for a visit, and she'll be too busy to spend time with us," he said quietly.

"Yeah. I figure we probably did it to our parents, and they probably did it to their parents," Theo said. "That's the way things go, I guess, but it doesn't make it any easier, does it?" He held open the back door of the squad car for him, and then slid in next to him; Fred was in the front seat. Theo watched as Fred leaned closer to the chief and said, "The boss isn't feeling any too good. Maybe we don't need the sirens today after-all." The chief nodded in agreement, and they drove to the train station in silence.

Not until they were on the Pere Marquette that Horace seemed to rouse himself. Movement, on the water or a train, always energized him. "What I can't figure out is how you knew that fellow with the gun was a federal agent," Theo said.

Horace snorted. "What makes you think I did? The truth of the matter is, I didn't know. All I knew was that he didn't kill Miss LeBeau."

"You mean?" Theo asked, his mouth open.

"Well, I hate to admit it, but once again we blundered our way through that thing from the get-go to the end," Horace lamented. "We didn't even come close to getting much of it right except for the business with the Meldens. And that was just pure dumb luck."

"Seems to me it's a good thing you didn't," Fred said. "Get it right, that is."

"And just what do you mean by that?" Horace snapped at him.

"Well, from what you told me about what the federal agent was saying yesterday, they thought they were hot on the trail of some criminals who were going to dump all that arsenic and other stuff into the water to kill off a lot of people. Looks to me like they did plenty of blundering of their own, so it sort of evened out, if you were to ask me," Fred said.

"Thunderation! You are right about that. They didn't know anything about the diaries or paintings, now did they?" Horace said, finally cheering up.

"And that means, with a bit of luck, the girls got the paintings off to the museum safe and sound, and no one knows a thing about the diaries. Maybe we're getting better at this detective business, after all," Theo added.

"Now, if you don't mind me saying so, doctors, you might want to think about taking up a new line of work," Fred teased.

"No!" Horace and Theo said in unison.

A Redcap met the Pere Marquette after it pulled into Chicago's Union Station and told Horace, "We were asked to keep an eye out for three men travelling together by the name of Balfour. That you gents, I hope?" he asked.

"Yes," Theo replied, "What's wrong?"

"Not a thing! No Sir! A couple of women, real lookers, but they got class so a man can tell they're no floozies you know, told us to keep an eye out for you and said you were to join them on the Empire Builder. Real high society ladies, you can tell. They said I was to bring you along straight away before you could get into any mischief. Pardon me for saying that, but that's what they told me I was to say. You gentlemen want to follow me? I'll take your grips for you." Before the trio could say anything, he was putting their bags on his cart.

"Say, I shouldn't be telling this to just anyone, but I figure you're men of the world, but if you see the club car steward, he just might fetch you a cup of his special coffee, if you know what I mean." The Redcap smiled, running the right index finger along the side of his nose.

"Seems to me a man ought to be rewarded for that sort of vital information," Theo said, pulling a five spot out of his wallet. "But say, you couldn't see your way to taking us straight to the club car, could you? We can find our way back to the ladies in the coach on our own."

"No sir! I got strict orders from the lady wearing a blue dress to bring you right along. And she tipped me extra to do it. Besides, they're already waiting for you in the club car!"

Theo growled under his breath, "Beatrix — again!"

"That her name? Well, her friend said she figured you'd try to pull a stunt like getting on in the club car," the porter added. "That's why I got orders to deliver you personal-like to them."

"Clarice," Horace muttered.

Clarice and Beatrix, along with the club steward, were the only occupants in the last car on the train. The moment Clarice spotted Theo she jumped up to wrap her arms around him. "You had me worried," she whispered in his ear. "All in one piece," he whispered back, "and very happy to see you again."

Horace and Beatrix looked at each other, uncomfortable and uncertain what to do or say once they got past, "hello." He waited until Clarice and his brother sat on one of the padded benches, then sat down, uncertain whether to stay where he was or move closer to Beatrix.

"So, anyone have any news to tell us?" Theo asked brightly, knowing full well they all had plenty to say.

Clarice went first, telling about the Palmer House and how they enjoyed the tea room, and how they had spent part of the day at Marshal Fields and had lunch in their dining room before going on to the big department store a block further down Michigan Avenue. "And, before you ask, I did not spend a fortune. You'll also be happy to know I had everything shipped back home so you don't have to carry it," she told her husband.

"So I don't see it, I think is what you're telling me," Theo chuckled.

"Beatrix, the paintings!" Horace asked, weary of Clarice's long monologue about shopping.

She offered a thin smile. "All went as planned. When we arrived I telephoned the young researcher of whom I spoke earlier. We set a time and place to meet, and he took me down through a side door and down the back stairs to his department in the basement, where

I gave him the paintings. As I planned, I told him that I was merely conveying them from a donor who wished to remain anonymous."

"And?" Horace asked.

"As I anticipated, he expressed great interest in them, but said that he would have to do additional research. All in all, I believe it means that the paintings are well out of sight for several years until they are verified as legitimate or forgeries. Just as importantly, they are now in a safe location. Because the museum will not want to have anyone steal their thunder, they will say or write nothing until they are certain about them. I made him promise to say nothing that would connect us with them."

"Congratulations, Beatrix. Well done!" Horace told her.

"And what about you three?" Clarice asked.

For the next few minutes Horace, Theo, and Fred stumbled over each other, trying to tell the events of the previous day, constantly interrupting each other, sometimes confusing Beatrix and Clarice.

"Well, I don't know about the rest of you, but I've been sitting most of the day. I think I'll walk up to the dining car and see what's on the menu," Theo said.

"Must you, dear? We're about to have some coffee before the other passengers get on," Clarice said. She nodded in the direction of the steward who brought a tray with a silver coffee pot, china cups and saucers, and some small cookies.

"Thank you," Clarice told him. "I'll be Mother and pour. I think you'll like this coffee. Beatrix and I had a cup a few minutes before you got here. You would like another cup, wouldn't you?" she asked her.

"Please," Beatrix smiled. "It's a wonderful blend called 'Old Grouse.'"

Even Horace was laughing at their prank. "Well, here's to us, the world's worst amateur detectives who bumbled our way to success again."

"And nearly got shot — again," Beatrix added solemnly.

They were still a half hour east of Madison, Wisconsin when the dining car steward came through the train, inviting passengers to the first, second, and third seating. When he came to the club car at the rear of the train he told Horace, "I saved six for you folks, if you are ready to have dinner. Table and a half." He looked at Horace and Beatrix and added, "Figured you two would like a chance to be together."

His comment to them was not well received. "You could sit with the others," Horace offered her. "I don't mind eating alone."

"Neither do I."

"That's a capitol idea, steward," Clarice said. "The three of us will sit at the children's table and leave the adults by themselves."

"You said that backwards," Theo growled under his breath.

"The one thing that still bothers me is that no one will ever know what you did, about the paintings and the diaries, I mean," Horace said while they waited for their meal. "Nor discovering the van Gogh green."

"I am quite comfortable with that. I prefer it. Anyway, it was preserving the paintings and the diaries that have the greater importance, and I do not need my name to be part of it. When the paintings are authenticated, they will be exhibited for everyone to see. That is as it should be."

"May we live long enough for that to happen. Might just be worth a trip to Chicago to see them in the museum," Horace said quietly.

"What troubles me is that Phoebe will never know your part in all of this," she said sadly, reaching across the table to put her hand over his.

"That part doesn't bother me. It's her not learning the whole story. If it hadn't been for her spotting those dead crows and writing to us, well, the paintings, van Gogh's formula book, diaries, everything would have been lost forever. I wish you could have seen her this morning, Beatrix, standing up in front of her whole school, quietly, clearly, convincingly giving all the facts and details about the dangers of eating apple seeds. She did a better job than some doctors."

"And she does not know the rest ..." Beatrix's voice trailed off. Horace shook his head.

"I've been thinking about it ever since. When I get home I'm going to write the whole story, start to finish. And then I'm going to give it to my attorney to give to her when I'm gone. She needs to know everything long after we're gone, that she was a part of something that is important."

To the surprise of both of them, Beatrix reached out to put her right hand over his hand that was on the table. "You have a good heart, Doctor Horace Balfour."

The Empire Builder pulled into the St Paul station right on time. There, it would take on water and more coal. A new engineer and fireman would take the train from St. Paul to Minot, North Dakota. An hour or so before that, it would stop to let the Balfours and Fred get off. St. Paul was Beatrix' stop.

"Twenty minutes folks. Step out and get some fresh air, but stay on the platform. Stay on the platform or you'll be left behind. Empire Builder waits for no one!" The conductor bellowed as he hurried through the cars.

"Here is where I get off," Beatrix said as she got up. Horace joined her. A glare over the top of Clarice's glasses made it very clear to Fred and Theo that they were to remain where they were. Clarice watched them through the window, the fingers on her left hand crossed. She wasn't fond of Beatrix. For that matter, she wasn't always very fond of Horace, either. But something in her wanted the two of them to have real joy in their latter years.

"Well, it's been fun," Horace said, fumbling for words.

"It has been a memorable experience," Beatrix corrected him.

"Oh, you mean the part about nearly getting shot and killed." Horace said.

"Yes. But the rest of it, well, it was fun, was it not, Horace?"

"We should do it again sometime. Go down to Saugatuck, maybe stir something up again. Well, I mean you will, next summer if you go to Ox-Bow, and I'll probably go down to see Phoebe again, and Harriet. Harriet, of course. Maybe we'll run into each other.

"I would like that. Yes, I believe that I would."

"Me, too."

"Horace, you know I fly solo," she said.

"Well, yeah, so do I," he added quickly.

"I flew with a passenger once. Just once," she said, looking at him.

"How was it?"

"Different."

Both of them felt relief when the train whistle blew, summoning the passengers back on board.

"All aboard folks, all aboard!" the conductor shouted as he walked down the platform.

"Well …" Horace said.

"I'll wait until the train leaves," she said quietly. "I remember what Fred told me that it made you sad that no one ever stayed to see you off. Sometimes, things do change."

Clarice watched them shake hands, then suddenly give each other a very awkward brief hug of farewell.

"Time to get on board, sir!" the station master told Horace.

Made in the USA
Middletown, DE
29 March 2019